THIS DARKNESS
GOT TO GIVE

by
Dave Housley

pandamoon
publishing

www.pandamoonpublishing.com

Jacket design and illustrations © Pandamoon Publishing
Art Direction by Matthew Kramer: Pandamoon Publishing
Editing by Zara Kramer, Rachel Schoenbauer, and Forrest Driskel: Pandamoon Publishing

Pandamoon Publishing and the portrayal of a panda and a moon are registered trademarks of Pandamoon Publishing.

Library of Congress Cataloging-in-Publication Data is on file at the Library of Congress, Washington, DC

Edition: 1, version 1.01 2019
ISBN-13: 978-1-950627-02-8

Critical Reviews

"Dave Housley has written a great bloody romp of a Deadhead psychic-vampire novel. As if, perhaps, Anne Rice and Hunter Thompson had met tripping at a Dead show and decided to reimagine Scanners. I enjoyed every page."
-Max Ludington, author of Tiger in a Trance

"Dave Housley has done something remarkable with This Darkness Got to Give. He's managed to combine a compelling procedural, a unique vampire tale, twin portrayals of loneliness and addiction, and a lovely, honest homage to the Grateful Dead and their fans in one outstanding book. I promise you - it's unlike any book you've ever opened. This is a novel you'll read quickly and never forget."
-- E.A. Aymar, author of The Night of the Flood

"A trippy, unique spin on the vampire mythology that'll satisfy Deadheads and noir purists alike."
-- J.L. Delozier, author of Type and Cross, and Storm Shelter

One way or another, one way or another,
One way or another, this darkness got to give.

Garcia/Hunter, "New Speedway Boogie"

Dedication

For Lori, my partner on this long strange trip.

THIS DARKNESS
GOT TO GIVE

Chapter 1

June 24, 1995. Washington, DC. Robert F. Kennedy Stadium

It was dark outside the van. The blackout windows were illegal but necessary, and since he simply couldn't travel during the day, it hadn't been a problem in the twenty-three years Cain had been on tour. Familiar sounds trickled in from the parking lot: somebody playing a bootleg that he identified as the Europe '74 tour off to his left; behind him, the terrible parking lot band that had been playing off and on ever since they'd arrived in DC two days ago. Scattered throughout, the buzz and chatter of Deadheads moving along through the lot, their calls advertising goo balls, T-shirts, doses, shrooms, burritos, cigarettes, beer. They shouted, sang, danced, fought, laughed, wept, chanted, chattered crazy, all of it a mere ten feet away from where Cain lay right now. It was the laughter that got to him. It made him nostalgic, then angry. It made him regret what he knew he would have to do later.

Time was important. The life, his very survival, it was all based on time. It would be time to go out soon. Already, he could feel it starting in his fingertips, something between an ache and a tingle. Soon it would spread—inward, moving up his arms and into his gut, up through his spinal column until his head filled with white pain, his body vibrated with agony and adrenaline, and there was only one way to make it go away.

As always, he listened through the parking lot jangle for the high-pitched voice of the one who had sold him his dose. The one who had known, somehow, what he was, had casually mentioned that these doses, his doses, were the only ones that would work on Cain, too. "I know what you are," the Dealer had said. "I know what it's like. I can help."

Cain hadn't said a thing. The man had read something in his eyes, or the lack of something, and handed him a dose.

Cain shifted in his bed, sat up. He listened. *"Shrooms doses shirts hey didn't I see you in Jersey dude that's my shirt…"* An endless stream of the normal chatter. But nowhere that voice he knew he would never forget: "I can help."

The ache was moving up into his hands, the tingle starting down in his toes. It had been three months since Saint Patrick's Day and the Spectrum and his dose, through the East Coast and down south and back out west and now back to the east and still no sign of the guy. Not that Cain would be doing anything different—he'd been on tour ever since he had gone through the change, almost ever since the band was touring at all. One thing he had learned: he wasn't very good at being what he was away from tour. But without whatever the guy had put into him, without that dose—so stupid—everything would be different. It would be normal. Predictable. Controllable. The same careful way he'd been living for the past twenty-three years. One dose, and everything had changed.

He stiffened. Somebody was approaching. Even after all this time, he wasn't sure if he was hearing it or feeling it. The books, the folklore was…inconsistent. Even what he had learned firsthand tended to fall somewhere in the space between self-help and rumor. He had been told, for instance, that some could fly. The older ones, the strongest. Cain had never seen it, had certainly never felt the release of leaving his earthbound tether and screaming through the black night like a hawk. He didn't know many of his own kind, had purposefully kept himself apart from the ones who tailed around the tour like lost moons looking for something to orbit again.

Knock, knock…knock on the side of the van. Footsteps. Then *knock, knock* on the other side. It was the girl. It was time. He sat up, put on his Birkenstocks and a tie-dye, cutoff jeans and a floppy hat. He didn't bother looking in the mirror.

The pain was moving into his gut. Along with it, the feeling of strength, something beyond the usual, something that felt like cocaine, what he remembered of it, like PCP the few times he'd taken it with the Angels, all those years ago. A feeling like he could do anything, like he needed to do something or he'd burn into himself like a black hole. He needed to get out there. He needed to do it, and soon.

The van door opened with a *whoosh* and shut with a snap. He locked the doors, checked them, picked up the chain from under the van, and looped it carefully through each door. He fixed the padlock and put the key in his pocket. Under the windshield wiper, a note. "RIVER," she had written.

Cain walked in the spaces between cars, avoided the major avenues crammed with people selling their wares, heads looking for a score, tourists watching the parade, searching for just the right shirt to take home to their straight lives.

A dirty teenager without a shirt grabbed his wrist. The kid smelled terrible—like sweat and weed and rotting flesh. Cain could tell he was dying somewhere. The smell was too much. "Hey, man," the kid said. He jerked his hand back. "Dude! Your arm is…" His glassy eyes came into focus for just a second. He took a few steps back. "No worries, man. Just looking for a few bucks, you know, but…" he backed up quickly, nodding his head. "Have a good show, dude."

"Show ended a few hours ago, man," Cain said. He reached into his pocket, grabbed a twenty, and held it out.

The kid just stood there blinking. He rubbed his hands together like they were cold. "Did they play Rider?" he asked.

"Not tonight," Cain said. "Cassidy, though. And Bobby sang…" but it was no use, he realized. The kid wasn't processing any of it. He waved the twenty again and the kid took a tentative step forward. "You should go to the doctor," Cain said. "Go and…well, just go."

The kid nodded, snatched the twenty and backed toward the main road. "Have a good show, dude," he said.

Cain continued through the parking lot, down toward the river. Have a good show, dude. He'd been to hundreds of shows, and every one had been a good show in one way or another. Nothing topped Europe, the early seventies, but these past few tours had been good, and he was relieved that it looked like he'd be able to tour for another decade, maybe, before he had to find a new home. Jerry played differently post-coma, but on the best nights he still had that shine, that tone, something about it different than anybody else.

Before the coma there had been rumors, whispers that Garcia had been through the change and managed to find some rich rock star way to manage the sun. It was ludicrous, of course, but he'd heard the same thing at one time or another about Clapton, Buddy Guy, Miles Davis. Of course everybody wondered about Keith Richards.

He smelled the river before he could see it. He walked between two vans and found the path, saw the light from the girl's cigarette bobbing in the weedy little stand of trees that lined the riverbank.

"What's up?" she said. "How far along?"

"Starting to cramp up a little. Need to soon," he said. He clenched and unclenched his hands. Soon, he knew, the motion would become involuntary. The back of his neck tightened. His head swam and he thought about how good it would feel to be released, to let go.

The girl stood, threw her cigarette on the ground. She stamped her foot on top of it and twisted, then picked up the butt and put it into a plastic bag she pulled from her back pocket. She wore khaki shorts and a white T-shirt with Winnie the

Pooh on the front. She had been helping him for the past few months and they had never exchanged so much as first names.

She pointed to the place where the path meandered along a squat stand of bushes and toward the river. "Same deal as the other night," she said. "Down that path, the little clearing. One dude, passed out. Bad shape."

Cain nodded. He could feel it getting worse, tightening. "Anything else I need to worry about, you think?" he said.

The girl shook her head. She put another cigarette in her mouth. "No," she said. "Straight junkie from what I can tell." She picked her beer off the ground and took a sip. "I don't think anybody's gonna miss him," she said.

Cain nodded. He fished around in his wallet, handed the girl five twenties.

"A hundred?" she said.

"Keep the change," Cain said, but she was already walking away. "Hope you had a good show!" he shouted.

"See you down the road," she said and made her way back toward the lights.

Chapter 2

June 25, 1995. South-central Pennsylvania. Chandler University.

Pete dropped his paper in the slot in Professor Peabody's office door and stood in the hallway. Could that really be it? College, over? He hadn't even meant to graduate early and now here he was, a few days and a piece of paper away from having to answer all the questions he had been hiding from for the past three years. Most people went into religious studies to find answers. He was dealing with a whole different set of questions.

And now a different set still: where would he live? What would he do? Where would he go for Christmas, even? Without the structure of an academic program, of department parties and the timeline of the semester and Padma feeling sorry enough for him to invite him to the odd graduate student get-together, did he even celebrate Christmas?

He stood in the cavernous hallway, realizing with a jolt that he had literally nowhere to go. The department still smelled like pipe smoke, although in his entire time at Chandler—four years undergrad and three getting his Masters—smoking had never been allowed inside the building. It had always been, for him, a mysteriously comforting smell, and he wondered whether someone in his family, back before the accident, some uncle or grandfather, perhaps even his actual father, had smoked a pipe. He breathed in the department's smell for maybe the last time: pipe, books, cheap disinfectant—and took some solace in the fact that even if the smoke smell wasn't so much a memory as the ghost of one, the faintest whiff of a memory; at least it was a happy one.

The photocopier started up in the department's waiting area and Pete wandered toward the door. Inside, Mrs. Lin, the rotund, bespectacled administrative assistant who had been running most aspects of the department since the day he wandered through these doors as a freshman, stood waiting for copies to finish.

Pete was suddenly overcome with emotion. Mrs. Lin. She looked exactly the same as she had on his first day of classes. There was nothing she didn't know. In many ways, she was the living, breathing, never-aging heart of the entire department. He realized with a rush that there was a very good chance he would never see her again.

He walked through the door and she looked up from the machine.

"Mrs. Lin," Pete said. "Well, I just turned in…"

The phone rang and she nodded curtly to him, picked it up, and shouted something in Mandarin into the receiver. She hung up the phone. "If you have to leave paper," she said, "find your professor door and throw through slot." She mimed the act of depositing a term paper through an opening.

Pete nodded and she bustled down the hall.

With nothing else to do, he wandered down the stairs and followed a group of laughing sorority girls through the massive old doorway of Glatfelter Hall and out into the quad. Campus had been emptying for the past several days as students took finals and headed back to wherever they were from, back to families and holidays and dinners, to friends and old hangouts, to girlfriends or boyfriends. They lived two lives, he thought—school and home—with the attendant trappings of each, the friends and lovers and couches and beds and posters. In this way, he was a simpler creature. He had just the one life, just this, his classes and his apartment and Padma and Mrs. Lin and Professor Peabody. His world was as limited, as prescribed and precise as the territory of a caged hamster.

He sat down in front of the library and felt the spring air—light and warm, like a cushion all around him. That's what Chandler was, he thought: a cushion.

A boy and girl walked by holding hands and he wondered what Padma was up to right now. Probably sitting around the kitchen table with her mother and sisters, laughing and drinking wine, like a scene from one of the romantic comedies she occasionally made him watch. She had never really explained why she had to leave so quickly, but he knew she would be in touch whenever her business in New York was done. He had no experience of his own, but he'd seen enough movies, heard enough about Padma's sisters to understand that families were complicated.

He looked back toward Glatfelter, looming like a castle in the dusky sunshine, a few offices still burning bright and warm. On the steps, a lone figure stood, looking straight at him. It was a man—tall, dressed in a suit and an old-fashioned fedora. He looked like a private detective from a black-and-white movie.

Pete stared and the man stared back. His fingers tingled and he squeezed his hands together. He had an urge to go see the man, find out what he was doing up there, but he put it out of his head. Must be somebody's father, he thought, checking out campus while their kid stuffed dirty clothes into garbage bags for the trip home.

He still had the apartment, at least. He would go back and watch movies for a few days, maybe start googling PhD programs. Peabody had gone to Georgetown. Maybe there was a place for him there. He could do worse than emulate Professor Peabody's trajectory. He turned back to Glatfelter and the man was gone.

He watched a butterfly drift along the well-tended hedges. So this was it. His last day as a student at Chandler. He owed the place everything. He had wandered in a broken boy, and even if he knew he would never be wholly fixed, the place had healed him enough that he would go out into the world and…do what, exactly?

"Nice night."

Pete jolted, looked to his left. There was the man in the fedora, hands in pockets, admiring the orange sky in the distance.

"Yeah," Pete said. He stood.

"Have a seat, Mr. Vanderberg," the man said. "If you don't mind, I mean. I'd like to talk a bit, if you have some time. And I think you have some time."

"How do you know my name?" Pete said. "Are you from the bank? The trust. It doesn't have a clause for graduation, I know that."

"No, no, nothing like that," the guy said. He handed Pete a card. "Carl Nutter. United States Department of Defense, Invasive Species Division. I believe you may be in the market for a job, and unless we're wrong about a number of things, which is frankly, unlikely, I believe we may have just the thing for you."

Chapter 3

June 25, 1995. Washington, DC. Robert F. Kennedy Stadium

Jenkins pushed at the corpse with his foot. "Same as the others," he said. "Motherfucker."

Crabtree looked around the periphery. He picked up a beer can, sniffed it, set it back down into the mud. "Fucking smells terrible around here. What the fuck are they doing to that river?"

"The river?" Jenkins said. "Really?"

"That's not how rivers are supposed to smell, man."

"We have another hippie corpse here. What is this, fourteen? Dead white male, two puncture wounds on the side of the neck. Severe loss of blood—how did they put it in the report? 'Lack of corresponding evidence at the scene of the crime.' Fucking Calvin and Hobbes T-shirt. Birkenstocks. I don't even know what these pants are called. Like genie pants? Hippie pants? Anyway, the point is we have a fucking serial killer out here somewhere and you're worried about the Potomac River?"

"The river is not supposed to be like this. The other thing, whoever's doing this, at least I understand it, you know? I mean, these things have to eat, right? It's nature. I look at it like, a lion got loose or something. You get these things out in the world and, fuck, man, of course it's going to feed. Get them out into the world and things are gonna end bad. We never should have…"

"Should have what?" Jenkins said.

"Never mind," Crabtree said. He picked up a rock and threw it into the river with a *thunk*. "Some other time."

Jenkins turned the corpse over. He fished in the pockets and pulled out a small baggie of white powder. "Another junkie. I don't know, this is starting to feel different to me. I mean, this is an unregistered, obviously, but it's not following the usual patterns, even. You think it's a junkie?"

"They can't even feel it, though," Crabtree said. "We know this."

"But why stick to junkies? I mean, look at this guy. This guy does not look like something I'd want to eat. Why not do like in the old movies, find some hot young thing and suck her blood? Does this thing have, like, a Birkenstock thing?"

"It's just eating, man. We're food. You're thinking too hard."

"I don't know," Jenkins said. He looked out toward the river. They would need to get the uniforms down here, get the body out before these hippies started coming down to piss or shit or get high, whatever it was they did to start their day. They would have to tell them the usual bullshit story, give them a reason for the FBI to be snooping around a Grateful Dead show. It was amazing what people would believe if you flashed them a federal badge and didn't smile.

He could feel the gears moving, the first almost imperceptible pieces locking into place. The junkie thing—there was something there. He watched Crabtree wandering around picking up beer cans and sniffing them, poking at cigarette butts, lifting up branches. What he expected to find was anybody's guess. Crabtree was a good agent, but limited. Point him in a direction and he'd walk through walls, but he wasn't going to come up with any new information on his own. He wasn't going to be much help until they could get a profile of whatever was doing this.

"This is fourteen," Crabtree said. "Grateful Dead John Doe number four-fucking-teen."

"I'm gonna call in the uniforms," Jenkins said. He reached into his messenger bag, took out a large bandage, and put it over the puncture wounds. They were tiny, and mostly obscured by the victim's awful beard, but there was no upside to local officers making the connection between the bodies and the puncture wounds and what was referred to in their training as "the folklore."

"Fourteen bodies of junkies on the wall," Crabtree sang, "fourteen bodies of junkies…"

Jenkins looked out at the river. Behind them, the sounds of people waking. Doors slamming, music starting up. He could hear the uniforms coming, quick bursts of siren as they made their way through the parking lot. These hippies must be terrified, he thought, and his mind flashed on a thousand drug boxes being stored in tire wells, glove compartments, stuffed into panties and bras and backpacks. There were a million little secrets, he thought, and hundreds of big ones, stashed all across this lot, and they would be here for a few days and then move on to the next place, and then the next. If the FBI didn't switch up, get some kind of leverage, they might never get in front of this, would be chasing the Grateful Dead like some kind of morbid, federally funded cleanup crew for the next decade.

"Let's get this poor motherfucker into the freezer with the rest," he said. "I don't know what we need to do, but we need to get ahead of this thing."

Crabtree picked up a stick and threw it into the river. He stretched. "How would we do that?"

"I know a guy," Jenkins said.

"Anything I need to know about?" Crabtree said. "Anybody?"

Crabtree's posture had changed. There was a look of concern on his face. So he did know, Jenkins thought. Interesting. "Just need to touch base with an old friend," Jenkins said.

Chapter 4

June 25, 1995. Washington, DC. Robert F. Kennedy Stadium

Cain had a system. He thought he could tell the opening encore song based on how long a break they took in between. This tour, they were playing some of his favorites: "Iko Iko," "Women are Smarter," the much maligned "Shakedown Street," even the too obvious but still joyful "Sugar Magnolia." For these, the break was short, businesslike. They came onto the stage confident, expectant, ready to shake the stadium to the rafters. Break was maybe eight minutes, ten tops, and he pictured them back there, sucking bottles of water and cigarettes and bowls, Garcia doing whatever Garcia needed to do to last another half hour or more. Other times, they took longer, and Cain could almost feel the drag in the energy level: they shuffled onto stage, looking like the aging men they were, waving sheepishly, Garcia trailing behind or even coming on a few seconds late. This is when they were more likely to play something lazy and obvious: "Dancing in the Streets" or "Good Lovin'," and Cain would slip along the back of the crowd, make his way to the exits and the safe passage of the van.

He watched the stage and waited. Roadies tinkling away at the piano, tuning guitars. All around him, the usual: a group of kids who he guessed were in college sat in a semi-circle, discussing the general merits of Bruce Hornsby, who had been sitting in on keyboards since Brent Mydland's death five years earlier. "I'm telling you," said a kid with short cropped hair in a tie-dye and cutoff jeans, who might be able to pass for a real Deadhead if not for his expensive watch and belt, "as long as they don't play fucking 'The Way It Is,' the dude is fucking great."

"No way, man," said a shorter kid with long hair and dirt under his fingernails, "as long as that guy is on keys, *everything* sounds like 'The Way It Is.' Fucking 'Rider' sounds like I'm in the fucking supermarket."

Behind them, another group entertained themselves by placing half-full beers on the torso of a kid who had passed out on his back, hands folded protectively over his privates. They giggled and high-fived.

To Cain's left, a couple sat cross-legged, foreheads touching. They held hands. "I'm just so sorry," the man said.

"I'm so sorry, too," the woman said back to him. They both wept openly.

A hippie passed by with two beers in his hands and a lit joint. He did a double take at the couple, paused, watched. "I didn't mean it," the man said.

"I didn't either," said the woman.

The old hippie sat down. His beard was gray and his eyes were youthful and live. Cain guessed him at sixty. "I have a shot of that, man?" he said, indicating the joint.

The hippie handed over the joint and the man took a long draw and then handed it to the woman. "What were we talking about again?" the man said.

The woman exhaled. Her eyes went dark and she wiped at her face.

"Exactly!" the hippie said. "Right?"

The woman exhaled, took another hit. Cain watched something in her eyes change—sadness to anger to resignation.

These scenes were playing out all over the infield, across the stands, twenty thousand Deadheads in maybe ten basic scenarios: high, drunk, asleep, dancing, singing, fighting, loving, scheming, tripping, and coming down. He had seen everything, had seen the same thing, again and again and again, all through the U.S. and even Europe, back in the seventies. At times, he wondered why he did it anymore. But then he wondered what other life was out there for him—what would he do? Register with the feds and live on Plasmatrol? Report weekly to an agent? Pee in a cup so they could make sure he was sticking to the government dole and not even supplementing with animals?

It was no way to live. At least he had travel. He had the sights and the sounds of life on the road. More than that, he had his decisions made for him. Where to next? Wherever the tour took him. It was better to have a structure, some kind of outside force driving his coming and going, than to be left to his own devices. He had seen too many people, after the change, not able to handle the possibilities. If you could do anything you wanted, without fear of dying, what would you do? The question could drive even the best of them crazy.

He felt the energy before it started, the way a fish might feel the tide coming in—a low tingle in his fingertips, a swelling in the crowd. Then he saw Bobby come onstage and the roar followed. How long had they been? Eight minutes. This could be good. Garcia came on next, then Billy and Phil and Mickey. Hornsby had snuck onstage somehow and was seated at the keyboards, fiddling with a microphone. That may not be a good thing, Cain thought. They had been playing "The Valley Road," a Hornsby song that sounded like the rest of the Hornsby songs, and Cain agreed with the dirty fingernails kid that all twenty thousand of them might as well be shopping in a mall the minute Hornsby opened his mouth.

After a while the band came back onstage. A few bumps from Phil's bass, some noodling by Garcia, Hornsby pecking out a run on the keyboard. They started up with the piano—thankfully it wasn't a Hornsby song—and Garcia began singing. One of the newer songs, one of the prettier ones. Cain wasn't always as up to speed on the new ones, but he liked this one, connected to it in a way that he knew was almost too obvious, and he reached his arms up over his head and pointed toward the sky, opened his hands and let his fingers splay as Garcia sang of death: *I will walk alone, by the black muddy river, and sing me a song of my own...*

Garcia sang, "*I don't care how deep or wide, if you got another side,*" and the sea of people sang along. Cain relaxed, breathed in and out, in and out. He focused on pushing everything up through his fingertips. For a few glorious seconds, he felt absolutely nothing, just the vibration of thousands of people in the same place, the thump of the drums, the heartbeat of the crowd as one living, breathing organism. It was as close as he'd been since the day he took his dose, as close to oblivion, or a higher plane, as he could get. He heard voices and music and a deep white noise that was playing just under the surface. And then he felt a thin break in the perfection of the show, like a static in his head. He didn't know how he knew but he knew as sure as he was standing there: the man who sold him his dose was here, in the crowd, somewhere close.

He was up ahead, Cain knew. Somewhere. He followed this sense through the infield and up into the second level of the stadium, then back down through the bowels and out as the band finished up the encore and the lights signaled the show's end. It was almost as if he had no choice but to keep on moving, like a hound on the trail of a dog in heat. His legs churned and he followed. People were in the way and he pushed, strode forward, edged past them in whatever way necessary.

Now they were making their way out to the parking lot, where the guy could go anywhere, could get in a car and drive, or walk right into a police station. Cain needed to catch up right now. Add to everything the feeling in his spine, in his fingertips: it was coming tonight and it was coming soon.

Cain pushed through the crowd that had gathered in the tunnel between the stadium and the parking lot. There were a lot of drummers tonight, a fair amount of dancers spinning through the puddles, fanning around the edges of the crowd that shuffled by on either side. Still, Cain could see the rough spots on the edges:

junkies crouched against the wall, looking for a spilled dollar or a "miracle" hit, hustlers scouting out a fragile teen or an oblivious frat kid. The scene had always been like this, he knew, ever since San Francisco, and long before Altamont. Find ten people handing out flowers, really seeming to believe in peace, love, and understanding, and chances were at least one of them was scheming, selling, manipulating, cheating right behind them, hiding in plain sight in their tie-dyes and sandals, wrapping themselves in the cloak of the revolution only to advance their own cause. Now, of course, it was worse. Now, the revolution had failed. Now peace, love, and happiness sounded as quaint and old-fashioned as a sock hop or a soda fountain. Even the true believers weren't in it for the long haul. They had degrees, trust funds, parents to fall back on. They were biding time until the call of IPOs and startups and internships became too strong, experimenting with life on the road in a controlled, safe kind of way, day tripping.

He remembered what that was like, the ability to change, to try a life on and then swap it out for another, to switch back to what you always were all along. But that was long ago, and he had made his peace with the change, had chosen to embrace those silly concepts, peace and love, as much as the change allowed. Until the Dealer and his dose.

He followed the trail through the tunnel and out along the walkway that went along the edges of the parking lot. For a moment, Cain wondered if the guy was making a break for it, and what he would do. It was what, eleven at night? He had six hours until sunup, seven if he was lucky. Getting stuck somewhere in the District of Columbia was not an option. He'd learned long ago that the best escape plan was to never put your sleeping or transportation situation at risk. The best plan was to rely on yourself and yourself alone. He turned into the parking lot and followed the trail along a random series of twists and turns. Was he even following a trail? He was following a…feeling. A gut instinct that the man who sold him his dose was up ahead, somewhere.

He paused, searched for the man in a crowd waiting for nitrous hits, Day-Glo balloons filling up with a steady hiss. A line of people were waiting for their balloons, standing about in various states of sobriety. Two girls sat on the ground, one of them crying into her palm while the other picked at a scab on her knee. A kid wandered out of line and another moved up. Tomorrow, most of them would be back at their lives, hungover, with a T-shirt and a story to tell. Would they remember the way "So Many Roads" gently segued into "Promised Land?" Would they even wonder where the band would be the next night, or the night after that?

The Dealer was getting farther away. Cain still wasn't sure what he was following—less a trail than a scent—but he knew it was diminishing, that whatever thin connection bound him to his quarry was moving further away.

And then it got stronger. Stronger still. It was like a vibration, a sound he could only hear with his inner ear. It was like the momentum of sitting in a moving car, knowing he was hurtling toward a horizon, but everything around him was still: the kid selling goo balls, the T-shirt stand behind him, the sound of Garcia's *Run for the Roses* album streaming out from somewhere. The feeling grew so steady that Cain was frozen in place. His arms trembled, fingertips tremored, softly at first and then increasing until his fingers were shimmering like hummingbirds. He stuffed them in his pockets.

Around him the parking lot whirled as usual. The sensation got more and more intense until finally Cain was frozen, his mouth set in a grimace, hands stuffed in his cargo shorts.

"Dude," a kid walking by with a dancing bears T-shirt and cutoff jean shorts elbowed his friend, pointed his chin at Cain. "Bad trip."

"Oh man," the friend said. He put a hand on Cain's bicep and the feeling was like a hot tea kettle on his skin. Cain shivered and shook with pain, and then surprise: he had been so obsessed with the Dealer, with the sensation of the man growing ever closer, that he had forgotten completely about the hunger. The kid was in his early twenties, clean shaven, with short hair and kind eyes.

"Dude," he said. There was real empathy in his voice, and Cain wondered for a moment if the guy knew what was happening to him. But how could he? Cain himself wasn't sure what the strange feeling in his chest was, why he was suddenly unable to move.

The kid produced a joint from his hip pocket, waved it in front of Cain's eyes. "Stay cool, man," he said. "You're having a bad trip, but if you stay in the moment, think good thoughts, it'll all be cool." He slipped the joint into Cain's back pocket. "When you're ready," he said. "This will help."

Cain tried to whisper a thank you, more for the gesture, for those empathetic eyes and the tone of real concern, a sound Cain hadn't heard in years, than for the joint itself. Other than the dose, his dose, drugs hadn't had any effect on him since he'd gone through the change. But he remained frozen, hands stuffed in pockets, twitching uncontrollably.

"Let's go, man," the kid's friend said. He was watching a group of spinners a few cars ahead, young girls that Cain guessed were trying on their roles for size. Maybe they would be at the next stop, Auburn Hills, or maybe they would go back to their summer jobs as babysitters, administrative assistants, lifeguards, and retail sales associates.

The feeling in Cain's chest was growing stronger and he wondered whether he was having a heart attack. He hadn't heard anything in the folklore about any kind of incidents, nothing physical, nothing like what normal people dealt with every single day. It was the one undisputed upside to life after the change. And yet, here he was, still as a statue and pain clutching his chest.

Then he saw the Dealer. He was a small man, hair tucked up and to the side in a way that would have seemed rakish on a movie star but just looked like a mistake on the Dealer. He wore wire-rimmed glasses and a red shirt tucked into khakis. He looked like one of the old heads gone straight, an engineer who decided to come to a show on late notice and didn't have any tour clothes left. He was staring right at Cain. He was unmistakable.

"Hey, man," the kid called out. "This your buddy?"

The Dealer laughed and nodded his head. "You know how it goes," he said. He slipped a Ziploc bag into Cain's waistband, nodded once, and continued through the parking lot.

The pain receded along with the red shirt. As the Dealer grew smaller in his vision, Cain felt his hands unclench, finger by finger, angle by angle, until he could put a hand on the kid's arm. His eyelids fluttered and he realized that he'd been standing the entire time without blinking. His knees buckled and he crouched on the asphalt.

"You run on ahead, man," the kid said, nodding to his friend, who wandered away immediately. "Let me get you over here out of the market," the kid said. "You okay to walk?"

Cain nodded his head. They walked haltingly between a station wagon and a low-slung Ford Probe. Both were empty. Cain looked behind them, where the market went about its usual business. Nothing out of the ordinary, just a guy having a bad trip. "Over here," he said, indicating a spot behind some straggly bushes. The kid helped him the few feet to the hedge. The pain had arrived in full, and his entire body now throbbed with it, pushing out, pulsing. He felt like he was going to explode, or shrivel into nothing and burn up like a slip of paper. The kid had such kind eyes. Cain had made it this far without hurting anybody. Or at least, minimizing the hurt with the help of the girl. How had they met again? He was surprised that he couldn't remember. "Sit here," Cain said. It was all he could get out.

"No problem, man," the kid said. He leaned over to ease Cain's descent.

"I'm sorry," Cain thought. He pushed up quickly, his strength momentarily returning, and bit into the kid's carotid artery. Cain had drank a liter before the kid knew what was happening, a surprised gurgle the only sound he was capable of before Cain pulled him to the ground and fed. In the waistband of his shorts, he felt the Ziploc bag. "I'm sorry," he thought, as warm blood rushed into his mouth, as his body unclenched and his head went blurry and then clear.

Chapter 5

June 25, 1995. South-central Pennsylvania.

Pete was washing the dishes. He watched his hands move counterclockwise one, two, three circulations and then transfer the plate to the drying rack. He picked up another plate and did the same. Then another. He was numb.

The United States Department of Defense, Invasive Species Division. And they wanted him to start next week.

He finished the plates and moved on to the bowls. The alarm on his watch went off. The clothes would be dry. He grabbed his keys and walked down the stairs toward the little laundry room. He had said yes without even thinking about it, with all these questions still churning in his mind, in his gut. He still didn't really know what he had signed up for. There was something about the guy, though. Nutter. He seemed so sure. He knew so much. The guy knew the topic of his senior thesis and what his final GPA had been and he'd made not-so-subtle allusions to knowing much more.

He rounded a corner and turned on the light. Two coin-operated clothes washers, one tumble dryer. A laundry closet was more like it. He paused in the doorway, stared at a spot on the back wall where somebody had written "BEEF" in permanent marker. It had been there ever since Pete had initially rented the room, junior year. Five years, he thought, of staring at that word while he folded his laundry, moved wet clothes into the dryer or dirty clothes into the washer. BEEF. Was it a nickname or a pronouncement?

He took a T-shirt out of the dryer and folded it. Then did the same with another, and another, until all his T-shirts were neatly folded and stacked. Then he did the same with his underwear. Then he took out all the socks and lined them up on the shirts, matched them one by one. He didn't understand how people could lose their socks in the laundry. How hard was it to keep your socks together? But then he didn't understand a lot of the things normal people complained about.

He put everything into the duffel bag and then paused. He took the card out of his back pocket: Karl Nutter, Supervisor, U.S. Department of Defense, Invasive Species Division.

"If you can start right away," the man had said, "we think we have a job for you. If we've underestimated you, if we've guessed wrong here, then…well, we'll just pretend this never happened."

"Why me?" he said.

The man had smiled. "If I seem blunt," he said, "it's only because this particular…position…is rather time sensitive. It's also because I feel like I know you a little. The department, because of what we do, we don't get this type of thing wrong very often, and we've been watching you for quite some time now."

"Watching?"

"Not like that," he said. His voice was flat, factual, no emotion in it whatever. "I find it's best to be straightforward. Somebody like you would only come to somebody like me, we would only get to this point, after a lot of work had been done already. Groundwork laid. Research vetted."

Pete nodded. "While you're being honest, I feel like I should do the same," he said.

Nutter motioned for him to go ahead.

"I have no idea what you're talking about," he said.

"Excellent," Nutter said, with no sense of irony or mirth. "I find that's best. If we're both honest, I mean. Here's how it works. You would have come up on a database at a certain point in time. You would have been assigned to a specialist, somebody who would have followed up with some more…personal research. You would have passed certain tests, qualifications, and then your file would have landed on my desk. Other qualifications passed and then, well, here I am."

"So…"

"Again, pardon my bluntness. You are an orphan, Mr. Vanderberg. No family. No girlfriend. No particular attachments to anything, I believe, other than Chandler University itself. On this last matter, I'm guessing."

Pete nodded. He stuffed his hands into his pockets. "You're not wrong," he said.

"Right. As of a few minutes ago," the man said, "you have a master's degree in religious studies. This is another check in another column for us, Mr. Vanderberg."

"A check?"

"Let's say that our business, the nature of it. It requires a certain ability to see the larger picture. To buy in without buying in, if you know what I mean. To be engaged without necessarily becoming involved. We find that religious studies majors have that ability. Generally."

Pete ran a finger along the card. Invasive Species Division. He shouldn't have agreed without knowing more. But what had he agreed to? To a meeting, nothing more. An interview. Virginia was only a three-hour drive and he had nothing to do. What were the chances? A government agency that actually wanted religious studies majors?

He looked around at the little laundry room. It had always been one of his favorite parts of the apartment. It was warm and light. It smelled clean. It smelled safe.

He sat down on a chair and pulled the duffel bag onto his lap. He took out one shirt and then the next, laid them on his belly, then his shoulders, then his head, until he was covered in warm, clean, perfumed laundry. He emptied the duffel and then reached for more, added a newspaper and then a stack of magazines. He wished for a beanbag chair or a sleeping bag. He wanted more, to be covered by a thousand shirts, for them to weigh him down and press him to the ground until he couldn't move. But as always, he made do with what he had. He felt the dull weight of his own wardrobe covering him like a blanket and he imagined that it was more.

He breathed in the fabric softener and he knew, more than anything else, that he was alone. Like every decision he had made since he was old enough to make decisions, he would make this one alone. He would go to Virginia, would talk with the agents, hear what they had to say, and then he would make his decision. He would do it all alone.

Chapter 6

June 26, 1995. Washington, DC.

Jenkins called the number on the pay phone again. Crabtree was either wasted or had gotten lucky that evening. Either way, he wasn't answering. He checked his watch: 4:45 a.m. Crabtree wouldn't still be out. Unless he hadn't come home at all. Shit.

From the gas station, he could see the whole scene: the dark stadium, the rows of cars, the lights and bustle of what he knew they called Shakedown Street, the action retreating as his eyes made their way back toward the darker recesses of the parking lot and the river where he and Crabtree had caught the body less than twenty-four hours ago. Right in the middle of it all, the black and white had its siren on, lights swirling, but no sound, throwing a blue and red funhouse light on the action of the marketplace, people coming and going, browsing and selling like a late-night hippie farmer's market.

He could hear drums. Every few minutes, a kid in a tie-dye or a skull and roses shirt would stumble past, either making comical adjustments for the man in the khakis and button-up shirt—no sense pretending to be anything but a cop right now, with everything that was going on—or so wasted that he didn't even register.

He tried Crabtree's number again. Nothing. Fuck it, he thought, they would hold the body, that was no problem, but soon it would be daylight and chances were that whatever had done this was already headed off to the next show, was most likely halfway up 95, or sleeping in some hotel bed in Delaware. He didn't know why—maybe the folklore had gotten to him—but he pictured it as a high-end hotel, the kind of place he would have never been able to afford to bring the family, back when they were a family, even for just one night. He tried to push the idea out of his head. It wasn't in the data yet, the idea that this one was rich. And bad enough as it was to start adding fiction into the data, it was worse to let these things get personal.

He walked through a series of parking lots toward the flashing lights. As he got closer, the sound increased: drums, noodly folk music coming from bad car speakers, people shouting about burritos or cigarettes or beer. There were people laughing and crying, pulled into knots in the grass or wandering alone, staring blank-eyed and purposeless.

A girl wearing an elaborate dress with dreadlocks and a nose-ring nodded at him and smiled. "Right on," she said. She had stopped and was staring up at him like she'd come upon a full-size Bugs Bunny. She put a warm hand on his chest and Jenkins jerked backwards. "Right fucking oooon," she said. "Be who you are, man. We all gotta be who we are, right?" She smiled and cocked her head to the side.

Jenkins reached out his hand and they shook, businesslike. "That's very true, young lady," he said. "I'm off to do just that." He nodded and she wandered back in the direction she had come. He thought about David. He was only, what, a few years younger than this girl? He found himself thinking that, minus the obvious chemically altered state, he might be happy if David wound up as well-adjusted as that girl. The boy was so wound up, always so frazzled, burdened with the weight that Jenkins carried now across the parking lot and toward the sirens. It was hard to tell whether it had gotten worse with the divorce, or with puberty, or if Jenkins just didn't know his own son very well any more.

The crowd had thinned by this time early in the morning, but there were still stragglers walking along the darkened lanes. The hippies gave him a wide berth, slinking off toward the parked cars or turning around, pretending to fiddle with something. Some simply stopped in place, or turned around and walked the other way. He didn't have to tell anybody who he was. Just like the girl, they knew.

"Be who you are." It wasn't bad advice at all.

He made his way over toward the siren, where the two uniforms blocked a crowd of twenty or so Deadheads in various states of undoing. An old man fumbled around the edges, his beard long and scraggly like a television wizard, his eyes burning like he knew something nobody else could. Jenkins wondered what it was with the drugs. Most of them, those same eyes. Burning was the only word he could use to describe them. Burning with what, he had no idea.

He flashed his badge at the first cop, a young guy who was clearly unsettled. Jenkins noticed a pile of vomit next to the body bag, a matching spot on the guy's tie, and another swipe on his pants. "Glad you're here. Finally," the guy said.

"Tell me what you know so far," Jenkins said.

"Kid over there found the body," the cop said. "Found it right here. Says he was looking for a place to sleep. I have no…well, no reason to doubt the veracity. Veracity?"

Jenkins nodded for the officer to continue. The guy was young, maybe the same age as the hippie girl he'd just spoken with. "This your first?" Jenkins asked.

"First body? No," the officer said. He looked at the crowd still milling behind Jenkins. "First like this? One of these, what they call the disappearing victims? Yeah."

Jenkins nodded. He was already thinking about how to get the body out of here, when he would need to call headquarters to get a van out. "What?" he said.

"Not my first, no," the uniform said, too quickly. An overcorrection.

"You said what they call the 'disappearing victims'?" Jenkins said.

The guy checked the crowd, leaned in closer. "Or other people call them the vampires," he whispered. "But seems to me if anything they're vampire victims, not vampires themselves." He made a pinching motion on his own neck.

"Who is this 'they'?" Jenkins said. So he was right that they were starting to catch on.

"Just people. You know cops," the uniform said. "Cops talk."

"Cops talk," Jenkins said. He nodded. "Okay, let me get started here."

"Thing did that was fucked up," the cop said.

"Thing?" Jenkins asked.

"Whatever did that wasn't human," the cop said. "Leastways no ordinary human."

"Motherfucker," Jenkins muttered.

"What?" the cop said.

"Let me get a closer look," he said.

Chapter 7

Cain drove. The DC Beltway had always confounded him and he'd learned to just get on the first exit and drive until he came to major road. It was shorter, often, than navigating DC's supposed grid or risking an altercation in the sketchy neighborhoods that surrounded RFK. So he circled the capital city until he hit 95 North, heading instinctively toward the next stop in Auburn Hills. Detroit.

He'd heard speculation that whoever had booked this tour had been high, and he had to agree: Vermont, New Jersey, New York, DC. That made sense. And then the southward line made a crazy loop west to Detroit, before pulling back to east to Pittsburgh and then bouncing back to the Midwest for dates in Indiana, Missouri, and the final stand at Soldier Field in Chicago. He had heard theories about the cross-country dates: promoters were getting tired of the scene, of the drugs and the kids and the arrests; that the band was losing control over management, that the tour had been booked around Garcia's rehab schedule.

He drove and he eyed the baggie in the cup holder. Ten doses. A quarter of a sheet, each square a little larger than a dime and stamped with a Superman logo. He had fought the urge to take one before he started driving, and also fought the urge to throw them away. He played the options in his mind. They could be more of the same, the Dealer's attempt to string Cain out or even kill him. There were plenty of reasons, he thought, why somebody might want an unregistered in their service. Or they could be the antidote, the key to turning his body back into what it was before his dose, a hungry but reliable and, more importantly, controllable force.

He saw signs for Baltimore and knew he should be looking to head west. He put a tape in the deck: a Garcia acoustic show from a few years back. "*You can look around all the wild world over, and you'll never find another honest man.*"

Signs were coming rapidly now: Laurel, Columbia, Baltimore 10 miles.

What the hell had happened back there? There was something between them now, a connection. But the Dealer had been in control, so it wasn't so much a connection as a leash. The poor kid was trying to help, thought he saw an old head in a bad way and was doing his karmic duty by getting him to a better place. A better place.

They would be looking for him. He wasn't sure who, but somebody. The junkies were one thing, but that last kid had been kind. He was somebody's son. Those straight white teeth, the sympathetic eyes. Somebody would notice, would sniff out an unregistered, maybe put the junkies together, draw some lines on a map, and figure out that the next time this was going to happen was Auburn Hills. He slowed. Of course. He got off on the next exit and got back on 95 south. He drove for an hour and took the first interstate headed west.

Chapter 8

Each of the folders held less than ten sheets of paper. They were manila, government issue, with pictures of the bodies stapled to the front. Their paucity was a testament to a life poorly lived. These victims had very little in the way of biography. Even allowing for the bureaucrat's language of paperwork, these men, and they were all men, had almost nothing—scarce tax records, off-the-books financial histories. Save for a few drug charges—the average victim had been arrested 3.3 times, 95 percent of the time on possession or possession with intent—these people were ghosts, barnacles that, when their tenuous hold on this Earth was released, left only the barest impression of having been there at all.

The bodies were ugly—gray and decaying. Jenkins had seen worse—children, hoarders discovered only when the smell reached their neighbors, but never like this, so many similar victims in one place, a trail of bodies, a data set so alike, it could only have one source. A shared source. An unregistered who had gone off the agreed path so far as to resort to its natural state, which is to say: a serial killer.

Except the last one. The last victim didn't fit with the rest. A twenty-five-year-old teacher, a regular citizen. There was something there too, some piece of information waiting to make itself known, but he couldn't figure it just yet.

Focus on the junkies, he thought, get the baseline and then let the shadows fill themselves in after that. His mind mapped the similarities, assembled data into comfortable columns and groupings. The folders were laid out in neat rows, one for each week. He had run out of room on the floor, and the two most recent victims lay on the windowsill. Each was drained of blood, for starters, with a puncture wound on or about the neck area. They showed signs of prolonged drug use—arms riddled with holes, teeth black and rotting, skin hanging off extended bones. They had very little in the way of personal effects—sometimes a few grubby ticket stubs, ten dollars in bills and change, along with a few pills or a baggie full of marijuana stems and seeds. Only half of them were wearing shirts or shoes at the time of death.

He had tried mapping their seat locations at the various concerts, but the resulting data would have only been useful to a practitioner of chaos theory, and if anything, Jenkins was the exact opposite. He knew enough to know these people were unlikely to even consider sitting in their assigned seats.

He had already done his time in the library, and knew the basics of the community. There were the Spinners, mostly female, who migrated toward stadium exits like mosquitoes toward a streetlight, where they would spin in circles like they were experiencing nirvana. The Tapers, who carried their own recording equipment into the shows, setting up near the sound booth or as close to the stage as they could get. The Old Heads, real hippies who followed the Dead like lost cats with literally nowhere to go. Wharf Rats, sober Deadheads, a concept he struggled to understand on a basic level, but they were indeed part of the scene and given the suspected biology of his perpetrator, they were a group worth looking at. The young people seemed to be either trust fund kids trying on their parents' sixties clothes or college kids taking a break from their summer jobs. Within each group, of course, there were endless variations—environmentalists, PETA activists, nerds, posers, fakers, and everything else. It was all data, all filed away. He had no idea when he would need this information, only that it would come eventually, when there was enough information for the wheels to start turning.

Jenkins was embarrassed to know these things, but the job was at least part anthropology. Whether you were dealing with gangs or drug cartels or child pornographers, you needed a baseline on the subculture—the groups, roles, mores, traditions, pressure points. It was all part of the job, the part that Crabtree would never understand. He imagined trying to explain the difference between Spinners and Tapers to Crabtree. He'd seen the look before—mid-explanation, watching Crabtree's face turn from amusement to disbelief to disgust to something more, something angry and dangerous, the part of Crabtree that had changed in the war, the part Jenkins knew enough to keep aimed in the opposite direction.

He smelled coffee and then remembered his own 7-Eleven cup on the windowsill, no longer steaming. Outside, the sounds of people arriving—the same grumbled greetings and reproaches that had been bantered about ever since the formation of the unit, most likely ever since the first lawmen had gathered in the first grottos, preparing for the day.

Crabtree would find him soon, and then the questions, the prodding, the man's insistent, steady lurch toward whatever was next would all start up again. Jenkins walked the rows, watching the pictures move by, allowing his mind to relax, take in data. A trick he had learned from Tibor. Breathe. Walk. Watch. Let the mind go free. Let your eyes be open. He wondered if the old man had brought this from the old country, or if it was something he'd come to on his own. Spend a few lifetimes as a cop, he thought, and you would put some tricks together. Breathe. Walk. Watch…

"Oh Jesus," Crabtree said. Jenkins hadn't even heard the door open. "This again? Breathe. Walk. Let your third eye figure it all out later or whatever. Shit, I thought you had a lead on this." He grabbed the folders off the windowsill and dropped them on the ground, sat down in their place. "How many more days you imagine you'll be walking around with your third eye open and shit?"

Jenkins stopped. He walked to the window and picked up his coffee. In the parking lot, the usual government-issue sedans coming and going. He wondered how David was doing. The poor kid's hair was never going to do what he wanted it to do. If he could only talk to the boy, tell him…oh, what was there to tell him? He would be back in Chicago soon, back to Kathleen and the life the two of them had made without him.

He picked up the folders one by one, putting them back in the order in which they had come to the division—first out, first on the pile. Finally, he pulled the last two victims from under Crabtree's butt.

"What's next, swami?" Crabtree said. He sat up and yawned.

"Next, I forget everything for a while," Jenkins said.

"Shotgun," Crabtree said.

"There's only just the two of us."

"Still."

Jenkins jingled his keys in his pocket. He needed more data, but he could already feel that somewhere deep in his mind, somewhere in the unconscious side, things were starting to click, data elements falling into columns, things coming together. Soon, he'd be able to point Crabtree at whatever wall was in their way and watch him run through it.

Chapter 9

June 28, 1995. Northern Virginia

The directions, the letter was careful to say, were to a building in Langley, Virginia, but not *the* building. How had Nutter put it? "The nature of our work is…sensitive. Different."

Pete mimicked the man's overly serious tones as he drove along the office buildings and fast food places. "Sensitive," he said. "Different."

On each side there were nondescript office buildings, names like E-max or Netcoders stenciled on sober looking signposts. There were a lot of car washes, chain restaurants, and big box stores. He passed a Bed, Bath and Beyond, and then a Target. More office buildings. He watched the street numbers getting larger, heading for his destination. "My name is Pete Vandenberg," he began. "I'm a recent graduate of Chandler University with a major in religious studies…."

No, that didn't sound right.

"I recently graduated from Chandler University…" But they knew that already. Would everybody here, he wondered, know as much as Nutter? Would they admit it if they did?

"I'm Pete," he said. "I think you know more about me than I do about myself."

"I'm Pete," he said. "I have no earthly idea what I'm doing here."

"I'm Pete," he said. "Maybe *you* can actually tell *me* who the fuck I am."

The office buildings were becoming scarce, replaced with used car lots and factories, the sidewalks lined with chain-link fence that looked equally suited to keeping people inside as out.

"Hi," he said. "Nice to meet you. I'm Pete Vandenberg."

There was no need to be nervous. Nutter had told him that. Either it was a fit or it wasn't, and what Nutter kept referring to as "the data" seemed to indicate that it was indeed a fit. What "it" was, Pete had no idea.

How did you get ready for an interview like this? Was there something he was supposed to do? Something he needed to prepare? But Nutter had said no, just show up. Show up and be yourself and that will be enough.

He passed a strip club and then another. Things were getting dirtier, gray, with litter lining the street. He allowed himself the indulgence of imagining what it might have been like to talk this through with a father and a mother. There would have been advice given, tips on handshaking and looking your interviewer in the eye, how to negotiate a salary, what the hell a 401K was in the first place. "An interview?" they would say. "Already? My goodness, son. We sure are proud." There would be a hug. A handshake. But when he tried to picture their faces, as usual, all he saw was a shining light, a blur.

He had no memories. No people. No matter what happened today, there would be no handshake, no clap on the back, no excited calls home.

Home was packed in his car—two suitcases and three boxes full of dishes and books.

The road narrowed to two lanes and he reduced his speed. Up ahead, a gray concrete building, three stories tall. He turned into the parking lot and found a spot among the sedans and wagons. He looked at the building. No guards, no signs. Just a number: 222. He looked at the letter. He was in the right place.

He checked his hair in the rearview, put the letter in his pocket, and walked to the door. There was a small lobby, roughly the size of the living room in his apartment. Behind a desk, a small man with a beard and close-set eyes worked through a crossword puzzle. Pete walked to the desk and the man stood up. "Nice to meet you, Mr. Vandenberg," he said, nodding his head. His hand was warm and sweaty. "We've been waiting for you."

Chapter 10

June 28, 1995. Outside Chillicothe, OH

Cain woke and was surprised by the quiet. It had been how long now? Twenty-three years of listening to the same sounds outside his window. Twenty-three years unregistered. Twenty-three years of day-to-day, hand-to-mouth, of "goo balls shrooms doses." It was twenty-three years longer than he would have imagined possible, back when he first went through the change. And he'd managed. He had survived. He had managed, despite the particulars of his diet, to make it twenty-three years without really hurting anybody.

And then he'd had his moment of weakness, and he'd taken his dose.

He rolled over. He lay still. No trembling in his fingers, no black pain crawling up his neck. Not yet, at least. What would he do if that happened? He had come to rely too much on the girl. Of course, he could do the scouting himself, but as always, the enemy was time. Simple math. The show might not end until midnight. The crowd might not disburse until two or three, and even then, a good portion of the traveling fans, those truly on tour, wouldn't actually go to sleep until four or five. That left a few scant hours of true dark to find someone nobody would miss, someone who just seemed a little less than the rest of them. And then to actually do the thing.

How long could he last in this hotel in—where was he? Maryland, or Virginia, maybe Ohio. He was not in Auburn Hills, or headed that way.

It had been so much easier before his dose, easier to subsist on cow's blood or squirrels, black market Plasmatrol or the occasional willing human, too stoned to remember or believe what had happened. Twenty-three years he'd made it, and then: "I know what you are. I can help."

It was oblivion he wanted. He knew this. It was the old feeling, the numbness. He hadn't felt anything but animal hyperawareness ever since he'd gone through the change. In this way, the folklore was correct. His eyesight was perfect; his movements were quick and easy. He didn't know how strong he was, or if there was really a way to measure the kind of strong he was now. It was animal strength, functional and raw. Nothing to be proud of or show off. Just a fact of the change.

But with the strength also came the rest of it, an acute sensitivity to everything around him that he couldn't turn off. That, too, was an animal instinct. He felt almost like an insect: his antennae constantly tuned to signs of danger, of approach, of any stir in the web of his environment. It made shows amazing. He was in tune with it all—the music, dancers, the air thick with smoke, the vibrations of thousands of individuals all gathered around one stage for the same purpose. It was the only time he felt even the smallest connection, the most basic sense of belonging.

But the rest of the time, it was terrible. He longed for the sweet oblivion of drink or drugs. The punch line being, of course, that he was no longer affected in the least by any stimulants or depressants, that until his dose he had felt acutely each of the seconds of his life since he'd taken the change, had felt them the way a grasshopper feels them, or a lion: sharp and immediate. All he had been looking for when the man had found him was a few seconds of peace.

What it had gotten him was much worse than anything that had gone before.

Chapter 11

June 28, 1995. Northern Virginia.

Pete stared at the front of the binder. U.S. Department of Defense, Invasive Species Division. It looked official enough. It had all certainly *seemed* official enough. But still, he couldn't get over what they had told him. It couldn't be real, but they were so matter of fact about everything. They had reports and spreadsheets and treaties that had been signed. He had seen John F. Kennedy's signature, right there in front of him, smudged and ancient and as real as the stains in the shabby office carpet.

On one hand, he believed it. They were very serious. Very convincing. From the lousy office building to the bad coffee, there was nothing about it that *didn't* smack of the middling effects of bureaucracy, no doubt in his mind that these were government agents in a government office talking government business.

On the other, as Nutter had explained, Pete had been trained to study belief, to examine the results of a particular faith the way an epidemiologist might study the spread of malaria in Sub-Saharan Africa. Religious studies were, by definition, the examination of other people's belief systems, the ways in which they were founded, the way they affected a person or group of people's manner of interacting with the world.

"Somebody with your kind of background," Nutter had explained. "Especially your particular...family background." He held Pete's eye for emphasis. "Is less inclined, let's say, to run out of the building and go straight to mass. To go tell his priest or his mother or some radio call-in conspiracy theorist. Somebody like yourself, say, might be more inclined to tilt his head in the way you're doing now, to listen the way you're doing now, and ask intelligent questions. Take all this information, decades and decades of research, back to the hotel and come back in the morning asking for more."

Pete stared at the hotel television. It was the largest he'd ever seen, but he could say that about the king-sized bed and the whirlpool tub and the wall-to-wall windows that looked out over the strip mall across the street. He watched the headlights move back and forth along the highway, supplicants migrating toward one fate or another. He walked back to the bed, where the binders and briefcases sat waiting to fill his head with knowledge.

Nutter was right, of course. He'd done nothing since he arrived in the room but read, digesting decades of first-hand field information about the United States government's battle against invasive species—or more specifically, Eastern European vampires. Nutter had outlined the path for him: the government's concern was traced all the way back to the Garfield Administration, when millions of Germans immigrated to the United States, among them either hundreds or thousands who had been through "the change." Of course, their numbers swelled as they made the voyage, and once they hit the heartland, they continued to grow. The species was inherently suited to the environment, or as Nutter had explained, "to any environment with oxygen and humans."

Some of the folklore was correct. They could appear to be superhuman, were stronger, faster, their senses as sharp as animals in the wild. They subsisted on blood—human blood was the best for them, "health food" is what Nutter had called it, but they could subsist on any kind of blood, including animals or the artificial Plasmatrol that registered vampires were given in shipments each week. "Mostly synthetic blood," Nutter had explained. "Also some anti-depressants, some other drugs in there, intended to, let's just say, 'keep everything in line.'" They couldn't go into the sunlight. They never died of natural causes and didn't experience pain.

In some ways, the folklore was incorrect. Their minds were human minds. The same ones they'd had as farmers or miners or middle school teachers, with all the strengths and weaknesses of human beings. "Leave some people alive for a century or two," Nutter had said, "and they're just as stupid as they were for the first twenty or thirty years."

They experienced emotion, although most became "harder" over the course of time, less emotional, less attached to people and things and situations, to anything, really. Loss was in their DNA. They were birthed in loss and they lived in death. It was that simple.

Pete opened the first binder again. *A Guidebook for the Management of Invasive Species, U.S. Department of Defense, Invasive Species Division, FY 1994-5*. Nowhere in the literature did it mention that word: "vampire." They were referred to as "non-human invasive species."

There was a knock on the door. Pete shouted, "One minute!" and hid the notebooks and tapes under the bed as he had been instructed. When he opened the door, a hotel employee wheeled a cart in, opened some stainless-steel trays, bowed briefly, and left the room as efficiently as he had arrived.

A steak, medium well, with Montreal seasoning. A potato with sour cream and chives. Broccoli. A Caesar salad. They had done their homework. A card was folded next to the cheesecake dessert: "Congratulations on your graduation. Welcome to the team? Invasive Species Division."

He cut a piece of steak, put it in his mouth. It had been far too long since he'd been able to afford steak. He had been meaning to go out, treat himself for graduation, but all of this had happened so fast he hadn't even had a chance. He cut another piece. It was the best steak he'd ever had. For the first time, he understood what they meant when they said steak melted in your mouth. He leaned back in the king-sized bed and chewed.

Could it get better than this? He wondered if he could fit the whole steak in his mouth, what Nutter would say when they found him in the morning. He would cut it into two pieces, stuff the first piece in his mouth and start chewing. Then he would crawl under the bed as far as he could go, get right up against the wall so he was bordered in on three sides. Then he'd pull all the papers and binders and the tapes and the CD player up under the bed. He'd put the second piece of steak in his mouth and push with a pencil, until it was all there, lodged, stuck. He'd let the juices run down his chin, or his throat. He would become short of breath, would stifle the panic, fight the urge to claw out from under the bed, to pull the meat from his throat. He would sleep.

But then he thought about Nutter, about how sure he was that Pete was the right man for this job. Invasive Species Division. He chewed and swallowed, put some salt on the potato. He noticed the carton of orange juice sitting off to the side. Tropicana. They knew things about him. The entire time he had been slogging through it all, high school and college and graduate school, through every prom he missed or night he spent alone in the library or the coffee shop, every Christmas spent watching the Yule log and trying to get gravy going from a single baked chicken breast, through each and every day, he had assumed he was alone. But he had been wrong all along. They were there, with him, a silent passenger as he made his way through high school and college and graduate school and now this, whatever this was. They had been there all along.

He rooted through the paperwork and found the contract. He had read it earlier, a lot of language he didn't understand and a few ominous passages about what would happen if he were "killed or transitioned to a permanent and separate state of being." He found the line for "Employee." He signed it.

Chapter 12

Jenkins just wanted to get out the door. "We're gonna be late!" he shouted up toward the bathroom. Silence. It had been three years since he'd shared a house full-time with the boy, three years since the divorce and Kathleen's move to Chicago, and every time he had David for more than a day, it was a constant string of surprises. "David!" he shouted. "We're going to be late for Aunt Jenny's. I have a briefing at eight! I have to run a briefing! About a murder. In…" he trailed off. There was no way the kid could hear him over the roar of the hair dryer.

This was a new thing: the hair.

Jenkins remembered what it was like. Around the same age, he had attempted to fashion a "feathered" look that certain kids in the grade above him had perfected. He had also tried the hair dryer route, along with mousse and the unconventional method of wetting his hair and then going to sleep with a ski hat carefully positioned to keep it in place. None of it worked, of course, and now he'd passed that same hair—chestnut and thick, chunked into unruly waves, impossible to tame—on to his only son.

The hair dryer turned off and then turned on again. He checked his watch: they still had plenty of time, as long as they didn't run into traffic, but even in Manassas, traffic was getting worse every day. When they had first moved here, when the agency had finally decided to get real about the issue and set up the Partners Program, the area had been an outpost, a small town. There were still farms then, a dairy where you could buy milk in those thick glass bottles. The commute had taken twenty minutes. Now it was a half hour, forty or forty-five if there was even so much as a blip on the beltway. There was always a blip.

He sat down and opened up his briefcase. The junkie thing was something. That he knew. Now he just had to look at the data, make the right connections. The most frustrating thing was that he knew he would do it—he would take the available information and figure out what it was telling him. The hardest part was the waiting. He needed more data. If he could fast forward, make whatever was going to happen just happen already, give him the data he needed, then he'd be able to put a dent in this thing, set Crabtree on his path and let him hunt under enough branches and rocks and run through enough doors to bring this case home.

And what would happen then, he wondered. More junkies alive in the world, following some hippie band from stadium to stadium? No, that wasn't what ate at him about this case. It was the incongruity of the whole thing. They just didn't act like this. Sure, there were unregistereds. There always would be. And that wasn't what was bothering him. Unregistereds? He couldn't give a shit. He wasn't a form-checker, or some kind of paranormal bouncer, looking at IDs and giving approvals, filling file cabinets with paper. But this one was not acting in the usual way. It was, he realized, acting in the natural way, the way they must have acted centuries ago. But it was flouting the law, the agreement that had been reached between the two sides long ago. If they all acted like that…the idea was too much to even entertain.

The hair dryer stopped and the door opened. David came hurrying down the stairs, shaking his head, his brow creased in a way that Jenkins recognized immediately as his own. The boy sighed, a disgusted sigh, and Jenkins flashed on his own father, distant and disappointed.

David hadn't had any more luck than Jenkins had had with the knit cap and his own attempts at feathering. "It's pretty shitty hair," he said. He noticed the boy jump, and then smile at the swear. He was overcome with an immediate and sharp affection for his son. He was so young. He should be carefree and happy. He should, but he couldn't. It was the same weight his father carried, the weight Jenkins carried. The people at the retirement community had started calling it depression when his father had really started to go off the deep end, but Jenkins saw it for what it was: realism, self-awareness, intelligence.

"Come on," he said. "Let's get going. It won't make anything any better to be late."

Chapter 13

The place looked like any other place. It could have been student apartments in a college town, a retirement home, low-income housing. It reminded Jenkins of the apartment he'd lived in after active duty, when he was doing intelligence training for enlisted men in Dover. Low, sand-colored buildings, three levels, six units a floor, eighteen young men trying to adjust to civilian life by drinking too much, chasing women around the Delaware beach bars, driving fast and experimenting with whatever the world had come up with in the time they'd been away.

He pulled up to the guard's checkpoint and got in line behind the resident shuttle and a few sedans that looked like official vehicles. There really weren't many differences, he told himself, between his own experience in Dover and what the old man was living with today. Both were semi-restricted, controlled environments. Both were self-elected. Both were…but that's where the similarities ended and the differences began.

He got closer and could see a few residents milling in the moonlight, standing idly as if they had just woken from a bout of sleepwalking and were still trying to figure out if this was the dream or real life. He showed the guard his badge and the guy, a young kid who couldn't have been too far past legal drinking age, scanned it like a box of fish sticks in the super market and watched what came up on his screen.

"Pickup or delivery?" the kid said.

"Excuse me?" Jenkins said.

"You're federal," he said. "Assuming you're picking up or dropping off."

"Well," Jenkins said, surprised to find himself overcome with anger. "As you can see there's nobody in the car with me here." The kid looked at his computer and nodded. "And, again, as you can see, there's no requisition request in your little machine there."

The kid typed something into his computer and waited while a little ball swirled. Jenkins watched. "Hangs every night around this time," the kid said.

Jenkins wondered what would happen if the stragglers by the fence tried to walk through the gate, if the kid would notice. "They're not necessarily cured," he said, nodding at the first row of apartments. "You know that, right?" The kid typed something and waited while the little ball spun. "You know that to even be considered for this facility, they necessarily had to have committed a violent act. Right? You know that? And 'violent act' for these people, you know what that means?"

"What? Yes," the kid said.

"You ever seen a violent act? *Their* kind of violent act?" Jenkins asked. He didn't know exactly why he was pushing the kid. Maybe seeing the walls around this place made him feel sorry for the old man all over again. Maybe he was getting impatient about so many bodies and so few leads. Maybe he just needed a good night's sleep.

The kid stuck his head out his window and looked at the entrance. He seemed disappointed to not see any traffic behind Jenkins. "I gotta…" he started.

"Going to see Tibor Havranek," Jenkins said. "Personal visit. I'll punch in when I get there, punch out when I leave. I know that our visit will be monitored, that there will be an armed guard at the door, that the man I'm going to visit has placed himself in this situation of his own accord blah blah… Anything else you need me to say?"

The kid turned back to his computer. "Whatever," he said.

Jenkins thought about pulling the kid out of his kiosk by the tie, about smashing his head right into that computer. He drove through the gate and parked in a corner, front facing the parking lot. Quick getaways. They were a hard habit to break, even here with a complex full of residents, each of them not only registered but willingly restricted, monitored, drugged into something less than a housecat. In the corner of the lawn, a young man stood watching him. Jenkins nodded and the kid drifted away, staring up at the moon. He was a shell, a former human in every sense of the word. It was a shame, Jenkins thought. Then he flashed on what he'd seen the previous night—that healthy young kid, a second-grade teacher, they'd learned, drained of every last drop in his body—and corrected himself: it was almost a shame.

He paused on the lawn and looked up to Tibor's window. He would have gotten the call by now, the official notice that he was receiving a guest, that one armed guard would be stationed at the door for the duration of the visit. Jenkins waited, watching the black curtain and the slim white slice of light between. He turned over his wallet in his pocket, thought about the data. It didn't match up. Something was wrong.

Finally, the curtain parted and a hand appeared in the doorway. A peace sign. Jenkins laughed. Fucking Tibor.

He made his way up the stairs and nodded at the guard standing by Tibor's door. "We'll be about a half hour," Jenkins said. He flashed his badge. "Why don't you go get a cup of coffee?"

The guard looked at him. He was middle-aged, had the look of a cop about him—that carriage, like he was just waiting to see what was going to go wrong next.

"You DC?" Jenkins asked. "Virginia?"

"I'm going to go get that coffee," the guy said. "You armed, I suppose?"

"What you think?" Jenkins said, but the guy was already halfway down the hall.

The door opened and there was Tibor. Jenkins was always a little taken aback at how they didn't age, a little self-conscious of the lines on his face, his belly pushing up against his suit pants. Tibor could have walked right out of 1980. He was tall and lean, with the same close-cropped salt-and-pepper hair he'd had walking a beat, with thick lips and blue eyes that for some reason reminded Jenkins of the old country. The nickname "Old Man" had started as a joke and become less funny with each gray hair, added pound, ache or pain that Jenkins accrued.

"Hey," Tibor said, his old-world accent putting a quick bruise on the word. "You look fucking terrible, man." He stood, as always, straight and tall, held his hand out to shake, a gesture that seemed oddly formal, old-fashioned, to Jenkins. As always, he didn't realize how much things had changed in the world until he spoke with somebody for whom they hadn't. Crabtree would as soon hug you as say hello, had recently updated his greeting to a high five, so it seemed always like somebody had just completed an alley-oop or hit a home run when all they'd done was stumble hungover into the break room.

"Welcome," Tibor said. He settled into a recliner. A coffee mug steamed on an end table, a series of folded up newspaper sections nearby.

"How'd you do today?" Jenkins asked. He settled into a chair and regarded the apartment. Same as it ever was.

"*Times* was easy. *Post* was…there are some things in here that maybe I should ask you?" he said, his voice rising with a question, teasing Jenkins, who had proved himself useless at crosswords back when they were still working cases together.

"Hit me," Jenkins said.

"Singer David of the stars. Five letters. Last letter may be…E," he said.

"Bowie. David Bowie."

41

"Ah fuck. David Bowie," Tibor said. Of course. Ziggy…"

"Stardust," Jenkins said.

"Ziggy Fucking Stardust," Tibor said. "Of course."

"And his Spiders from Mars," Jenkins said.

Tibor raised his eyebrows. This had been a running joke. Everything getting more and more silly. Tibor had lived through the first six decades of the century with only mild annoyance, but the sixties and the amazing Technicolor fluidity of that era had driven him crazy. "Hundreds of years things are pretty much the same," he would say, "and then all of a sudden…" and he would wave his hands around and make silly noises, the only way he could think to indicate the depths to which society had sunk.

Like most of his species, Tibor kept no photographs, no souvenirs, the slow march of history having worn down any sense of nostalgia that may have lingered. Jenkins always thought of him as belonging to the industrial revolution, or maybe the time just before, the last time, maybe, when a cop on a beat required no technology save a nightstick to do his job, no more special training than the streets would have provided an observant and willful boy before he was out of high school.

"So," Tibor began, "how is David? He must be, what, fifteen?"

"He's fine," Jenkins said.

"And no wedding ring," Tibor said.

Jenkins held his hands up in a useless gesture.

"It happens," Tibor said. "And you haven't slept much in the past few nights." He said it flat, no judgment. A cop's habit, if anything.

"Got something that doesn't add up," Jenkins said.

Tibor nodded, sipped at his cup. Jenkins wondered whether it was coffee or Plasmatrol. He remembered the old man drinking the two together, the way other cops might throw a splash of whiskey into a coffee, when it had first come out.

"Unregistered. Feeding every other night. On the Grateful Dead tour."

"They are still around," Tibor said it flat, again just notching an observation, adding data to the equation that Jenkins knew was building in his head. "The fucking Grateful fucking Dead."

"Not exactly your thing, I know," Jenkins said. Tibor shook his head, waved his hands in the air in what Jenkins knew was as far as he would come to a ridiculous gesture.

"I had this girl down there, hippie girl, say the most amazing thing to me the other day. Down there at the crime scene. Which reminds me: so the thing is, this unregistered seems to be on the tour. They do that still, tour around with the band, go to all the shows—"

"Still?" Tibor said. "Still with that same band? Maybe it's true what they said about…whatshisname?…Garcia?"

"He ages, though," Jenkins said. He had heard this theory before, more than once over the past week. "He's aged. Gray and fat, same as the rest of us." Tibor nodded, a concession. "So anyway, whoever this is, they're killing junkies, people nobody will miss. Not much of a trail, you know."

"Taste is awful," Tibor said. He took a sip of his drink and then placed it back on the table.

Jenkins paused and regarded his friend. There were aspects of Tibor's life, what it really meant to go through the change, to live that way, that Jenkins would never understand.

"Regardless. This last one. It fits the MO right up to the victim. This one was young. Fucking second-grade teacher, believe it or not. A regular citizen. And there's still people around, just off this main part of the parking lot where they buy…I don't know, this isn't going to make any sense at all, like grilled cheeses and T-shirts and shit."

Tibor sat up. Jenkins could see his wheels turning, the old cop comparing one data point against the others. "Can you get me the file?" he asked.

Jenkins pulled the binder from his bag, dropped a copy on the table next to the crosswords. "A new riddle for you to figure out," he said.

"So you never finished your story," Tibor said.

"What? The ending is he killed the guy and we can't find him."

"No," Tibor shook his head, smiled an indulgent smile. "About the girl from the concert. She said something amazing to you?"

Jenkins stood. "Be who you are," he said.

"Be who you are," Tibor said.

"That's what she said to me. Held her hand right there on my chest and said, 'be who you are.' What do you make of that?"

"What do I make of it?" Tibor said. He waved around the small apartment. "What the fuck do you think I'm doing in this place, my old friend?"

43

Chapter 14

June 30, 1995. Pittsburgh, PA. Three Rivers Stadium.

Padma waited in line for the pay phone. It was late and the girl ahead of her was crying, begging somebody on the other end to send money, to come get her, to kick the ass of somebody named Gregor.

It had been a long night. She'd scoured the lot for the van, had walked for hours then had finally gone into the show, where again she found no sign of the biker. He was either hiding or had taken off. The only surprising thing about that, she realized, is how much sense it made. Maybe he was smarter than she thought.

The girl slammed the phone and walked off in a huff and Padma picked it up, entered the numbers and the calling card information, and waited while the phone rang.

"It's me," she said to the answering machine. "He's taken off. The biker, that is." She sighed. "Actually," she said. "As far as I can tell, they've both taken off."

Chapter 15

June 30, 1995. Outside Chillicothe, OH.

Cain could feel it coming on. Not now, he thought. Not in this hotel in the middle of nowhere. It can't be happening now. Was it happening more frequently? Had the contact with the Dealer somehow made it even worse?

He paced the narrow area between the bed and nightstand. Four steps toward the window. Four back to the door. The tingling had started on the road and he was lucky to find the motel before the pain had started up in his spine. He'd paid the clerk in cash and retreated to the room without a word. He was pretty sure nobody had seen him.

One, two, three, four steps to the window. One, two, three, four back to the door.

Not now.

The pain welled up his spine, bringing with it the familiar hunger, something deeper, more primal than he'd ever experienced before the turn, or even before his dose. Something bigger than him.

He looked out the window. Nothing but a highway and a low, industrial building ringed with chain link.

One, two, three…he looked again at the doses on the nightstand. So many questions.

Would it cure him or kill him? Either would be fine, at this point. What he couldn't risk is the possibility that it would somehow enhance the hunger, that the episodes would come with greater frequency, require more blood, before they would subside.

What was it that bound him to the Dealer, the connection as sure as an umbilical cord the closer they got to one another?

He sat down on the bed, lay back and looked at the water-stained ceiling. Motel 6. He had spent a weekend in a Motel 6 outside La Jolla sometime just before the change. Three Angels and a girl they'd picked up in a bar. An eight ball and two thirty-packs of Coors. The girl had started off cocky, a fireplug. By the end of the weekend, she was begging Cain to kill her, and he'd calmly obliged.

Cain wasn't proud of what he'd been before the change.

After the change, he'd done all the soul searching, the normal things, went through the stages of grief. Finally, he'd come out the other side resolved to look at the change for what it really was: a new start. The thing that got most people was the fact that there wasn't an ending. Cain had done enough, the drugs and the crime and even what they'd done to that girl in that Motel 6, and he knew that if he was going to be able to live with himself forever, whatever that meant, he'd have to put that part of his life behind him for real, start working on living the right way. Or as close as his new biology would allow to it.

Pain wormed up his spine and into his head. The thing was overtaking him and his fingers trembled, his legs shook. He wondered what the girl was doing right now. Probably halfway to Indiana, stepping through campgrounds or under bridges looking for somebody Cain could feed on, somebody nobody would miss. This is as close as he got lately to living the right way.

The pain increased, swelled in his head until he thought it would explode. But it wouldn't explode. This was the punch line, the eternal joke of his condition. He stumbled to the window. No traffic on the highway. He looked at the doses. If only they would kill him.

That kid. It was not the right way. But the right way had gone out the door the moment he took his dose.

He stood, stuffed the doses and his keys into the overcoat, and stumbled toward the door. The stairs seemed massive, each one a treacherous cliff. His vision was blurry, the hallway a gauzy mass of grays and yellows. He pushed the door open and lurched in the direction of the desk.

"Hey, man," the clerk said. "Partyin' a little up there, huh?" He was a portly little man with a ponytail and thick glasses. He had a hint of a southern accent.

Cain steadied himself on the desk. He didn't even look behind him. "Sorry," he said, and he leaned over the desk and let his mind go blank and felt his teeth digging deep into the guy's neck.

* * *

Cain drove the speed limit, as always. He drove south for an hour and then headed east. He didn't even know what road he was on, just drove. He registered small motels, dive bars, convenience stores. Eventually the road opened up and he passed horse fences on both sides. It was 4 a.m. He had an hour, maybe two, before sunup. As he drove, the doses rattled and shook on the dashboard.

He pulled out a baby wipe and cleaned his hands again. The baby wipes were an actual improvement—one of the few real signs of progress he'd seen over the past fifty years. They were clean, self-contained, could easily be disposed.

He gritted his teeth at the fact that he had a need for this kind of item. It was not him. Again, he thought of the Dealer, looked at the doses.

Up ahead, a police car, headlights on and siren off, sat waiting on the side of the road. Cain checked the speed limit, held the wheel with one hand while he moved the doses into the glove compartment. He was probably still in Virginia. Not inconceivable that his California plates would get him pulled over, that he'd get a citation for the blackout windows. Worst case scenario, they start rooting around in the van's garbage, stuffed with baby wipes smeared with the hotel clerk's blood. He wondered if they had a special prison for people who had gone through the change, a windowless holding cell, maybe, until they shipped him off to the federal facility he'd heard stories about. Lockmoor. An all-vampire secure facility and testing center. He had always thought it was a rumor, a dark fairy tale. Now he was one bored local cop away from finding out if it was real or not.

His body tensed, readying itself for…what? He was capable of anything. Pull the cop's head off and drink every last ounce of blood in his body? Bite his carotid and feed until his body went limp, then stuff it in the trunk of his car and head south? He could do anything. But he wouldn't. He wouldn't. He was not that kind of person. Not anymore.

He drove past the police car, maintained his speed, careful to stay as straight as possible. The worst thing he could do right now was swerve, give any indication that he was a drunk on his way home from the many dive bars he'd passed. The police car remained still.

He flashed on the hotel clerk's body, graying and jammed into the linen closet, awkwardly splayed on top of a mop and some boxes. Could he still say he wasn't that kind of person?

In his rearview, the police car pulled out, turned on its lights. Cain's entire body tensed. The car executed an awkward U-turn across both lanes and headed in the other direction. Cain waited until he couldn't see the lights anymore and then pulled over in the parking lot of a run-down video store. He got out of the car and drew his breath. His body was shaking. His teeth were sharp and ready. Was he disappointed?

What had the Dealer put into him? What was it that was propelling him away from his neat and orderly life of safe choices and careful plans? Was it the drug? Or was it there in him all along—the ghost of the man he'd been before the change—and the Dealer had simply brought it to the surface?

He remembered a time from long ago, before the change. An afternoon at the beach with a woman he had been dating. A different one than the rest, with an office job, an education. She was brunette and smart, with long legs and a sarcastic sense of humor that was unusual in those days. They had met at the laundromat, as opposed to the bar, which is where he and the rest of the Angels had met most of their women. Cain could tell that with his shoulder-length hair and leather pants, his motorcycle boots and tattoos, he was an exotic object for her, a talisman of everything that was happening at that time in San Francisco. For all her jokes and flirting, she was living a straight life. Cain was not. He had been interested in her for a while, maybe even a little bit in love. And now he couldn't remember her name.

Angela, maybe? Angeline? He did remember the daughter. Sophie. At that time, even in the sixties San Francisco, an unwed mother was scandalous. No wonder, he thought, she had to resort to him for some male companionship. He had never spent any time around children, and was frankly nervous about the prospect. But the girl had been a wonder. She was smart, friendly, questioning. When Cain told her that the waves were caused by sea monsters, she had screwed up her face into a question mark, slowly shaken her head and said, "I don't think so." He suggested making sand castles and she had created a sand version of Alcatraz instead. When she finally tired and lay down on the blanket, Cain in the middle with a woman on each side, one a tiny little replica of the other, both of them smart and unwilling to let him get away with any of his usual bullshit, he had been as potentially happy as he had ever been in his life. He knew, even then, that there would be something that would come along to knock this little family idea off his shoulder, and it had happened soon enough with his lost weekend, the DEA agent and the girl and then, soon after, the change.

He looked at the moon, graying with the coming morning. He wondered what became of the woman, of her perfect little daughter. The girl would be, what, thirty now? Thirty-five?

This is not who I am, he thought. If he stayed out here, how long would it take for him to die? Would he even be able to fight it off, once the sun came out? He'd heard of it being done. The key, they said, was chains. Strong chains, and enough of them to prevent even a desperate vampire from escape. He imagined it: a few minutes of struggle, burning flesh, the amazing spectacle of the sun on his face, and then sleep.

Nobody really wanted to be like this. Some, maybe, but those were sociopaths to begin with, outcasts, serial killers, or simpletons who had little trouble making the transition. He thought about laying down in the gravel, chaining himself to the video store and waiting for sun. All of this would be over. He thought about the hotel clerk, the doses jangling in the glove compartment, the Dealer.

He got back in the car, turned around in the direction he'd come, and drove west.

Chapter 16

July 1, 1995. Northern Virginia.

Jenkins pulled the dog along the sidewalk. There was a bag in his pocket but, as always, he intended to shoo Sandy as close to the school as possible. The school was public property, and Jenkins had no trouble making peace with the idea that his taxes were paying for somebody to pick up that shit for him. "Come on, Sandy," he said, "let's go, boy. Let's go." He yanked, ran along with the dog as he sniffed a line of hedges and then squatted just over what Jenkins thought was probably the line for school property. Yes, he thought. Thank goodness for small victories.

"Good boy."

He looked around at the neighborhood. Most houses were dark, light seeping out of a few windows. Of course, the Slaters were awake. The blue light of the television bounced around the living room. He could hear them in there, arguing as usual. Their music was a little too loud. Like all registereds, their yard was immaculate. The city mowed twice a week, no matter the weather. Jenkins thought of his own lawn, ragged and six inches high. To have the city come mow while you slept in your sealed-tight bunker in the basement, Plasmatrol deliveries once a week, government subsidy for the mortgage. The life of a registered vampire sounded pretty good some days.

Tonight he would go home, feed the dog, call Kathleen's place in Chicago to talk to David, who would in all likelihood not be there, or at least would not want to talk. Then he would make a Salisbury steak TV dinner, pull out his notes, and pour over them until his six-pack was gone. If there was a game on, he would listen to it. Then he would brush his teeth, go to bed, wake up, and do it all over again. Thank goodness for Sandy.

He thought of Tibor. He had done the right thing. Put himself in a place where he was controlled, where the possibilities of his condition were limited. "Be who you are" is what the girl had said, and if anything, Tibor knew who he was, knew it better than anybody, and had made the hard decision that what he was needed to be managed. Jenkins knew instinctively that, if he was in the old man's shoes, if he had slipped like the old man had slipped, he would make that same terrible decision.

Still, he could never quite reconcile the old man and his crosswords with the detective who had trained him, couldn't quite shake the idea that there was something owed, some kind of unsaid agreement between them that he was not living up to. Every time he visited, he waited for Tibor to mention it, to put the cards on the table, but despite his modern appearance, Jenkins knew the old-world ways were hard in the old man, and he would never ask for something that he believed was simply owed.

The dog picked up the empty remainder of a juice box and Jenkins pulled it out of his mouth. Labs would eat anything. Anything at all.

He assembled the data again in his mind. He could hear the old man's voice in his head, his thick accent: "Just put the pieces together. The information is in the data. It ain't that hard."

He had sixteen bodies. Fourteen of them junkies. All of them killed on this particular tour. Bodies found the next day in out of the way locations. Very few of them had family or friends. Most were just drifting along, either on tour or straight junkies, they thought, hanging around and hoping to scrounge up a high. Fourteen bodies that matched that description. And then this last one was younger, a second-grade teacher. Found in what was, for all intents and purposes, given that this was a Grateful Dead show, broad daylight. It was the equivalent of killing somebody in the middle of DuPont Circle. The other one, the hotel clerk, wasn't exactly a second-grade teacher, but by all accounts, wasn't a junkie either. He was nowhere near a Dead show.

Maybe this was a different killer. But the puncture wounds matched up. It wasn't a guarantee—puncture wounds were a 90 percent match—but it was a good indication that they were dealing with the same one, that something had gone different, off the tracks, and he was changing up his operation for some reason. But it didn't feel like a conscious change. It felt desperate.

The dog made a guttural sound. He leaned close to the grass, coughed a piece of plastic out of his mouth. A chewed-up piece of Tupperware or some kind of wrapper. He picked it up again and chewed. Jenkins pulled the thing out of his mouth, threw it behind the fence. Sandy looked at him like he'd just tossed a steak in the garbage can.

He turned the data over again in his head. The timeline was static, each murder and its attendant particulars matching roughly the same parameters, data filling the same columns in the same way, until a few days ago.

The dog found another piece of something and chewed. Jenkins knew he should pull the thing out of its mouth, but he also knew he was onto something with this line of thinking. What had changed? The vampire? But that didn't happen. That was the whole deal—they didn't age, decay, die, any of it. But this one. Something *had* indeed changed.

The dog started up again, coughing, gurgling. Jenkins grabbed at his mouth, yanked until he pulled a flattened plastic bottle out of the dog's mouth, along with a slick pool of bile.

That was it. The vampire was acting like an animal. Through all the years, they'd been convinced that these things were somehow elevated, above humans somehow. The folklore didn't help, with its urbane and tortured protagonists.

He thought of the old vampire sitting in his self-imposed exile. The man knew more about detective work than anybody Jenkins had ever met. Everything Jenkins knew—the data, the watching, the listening, carefully assembling the pieces until they told you a story—it had all come from the old man.

But still, the old man knew. He was an animal. He couldn't be trusted. After the incident on the Mall, he hadn't even stopped by his own apartment, had simply walked into the office and tendered his badge, filled out the post-shooting report—the closest the office had to what had actually happened—and had driven right to the facility and checked himself in.

"Be who you are," the girl had said. Tibor was an animal. This thing was an animal. It was acting like an animal. But not just that. It was acting like an animal that had gotten sick.

Chapter 17

July 2, 1995, Noblesville, IN. Deer Creek Amphitheater.

Before he even got to the show, he noticed them. First, the stickers: dancing bears, skulls and roses, a handprint with half a middle digit. They were on VW buses and Jettas and BMWs, first a trickle and then, as he got closer to the stadium and traffic started to slow, it seemed like every car on the highway was full of Deadheads on their way to the show. Pete glanced at himself in the mirror. They had deemed the hair too short to do anything with, so they'd advised him to wear a bandana. He hadn't shaved since accepting the position, a full week, and he scratched at his neck, pulled at the itchy hemp necklaces they'd given him. He turned up the volume on the CD player—*Europe '72*, an album he was growing to actually like, despite himself—and nodded along with the song, a sped-up country western tune about a kid and his uncle on a robbing spree in the old west. The music was not what he thought it would be. He had expected something heavy, weird, something more like the Zappa albums they'd listened to in his music class freshman year. This was folk, country, a little bit of random spacey stuff thrown in there for flavor, maybe, but it was music he imagined you could play for your parents. He liked it.

Traffic ground to stop-and-go and he looked over at the car next to him— three hippie girls who couldn't have been much older than eighteen. They were laughing and nodding along, the head bob somewhere between a dance and a confirmation. Pete waved, attempted a version of the same nod, lifted his hand in a greeting. The girl behind the wheel lowered her window. She looked straight ahead and Pete realized that she was edging closer to his lane. "Hey, man," she shouted through the window.

"Hey!" Pete said.

"You got tickets?" she said. "Extras?"

They had counted on this scenario, but not until he actually got to the show. "Look around," Nutter had counseled. "Find the Deadheadiest Deadhead you can. Somebody who looks like they haven't paid a bill in years. That's who you want to connect with."

"We need a miracle, man," the girl said. She reached into the back seat, then turned forward and took a drag from a joint. Pete knew this was coming, too, but the juxtaposition—while driving?—still threw him for a loop. She smiled. She was pretty, with long chestnut hair and eyes that he guessed were sleepy when she wasn't high, too. Pete realized how long it had been since he'd even talked with a woman. He wondered what Padma was up to right now, what she would think if she could see him.

"I have three tickets," Pete said. "Two extras if you want them."

"Sweet!" the girl shouted.

"Sweet," Pete said. The word felt foreign but nice in his mouth, like he was trying out a greeting in a foreign tongue.

"I'm Sunny," the girl said. "Follow us."

Traffic was picking up and he could see the stadium, a concrete hulk in the distance. He watched as the girl pulled in front of him and they made their way along with thousands of other cars. Sweet. He was now the kind of person who said "sweet!" in regular conversation, in moving cars, on the way to a Grateful Dead show. It seemed like a pretty good start.

Chapter 18

Cain moved aside the van's heavy curtains and peeked out. Cornfields rolling gently into the distance, a half-moon framed against the blackening sky. Parking the van here, even on such an isolated road, behind a stand of trees, had been a stupid risk. He couldn't run like this anymore, floating around like a teenager who had just taken his first mushrooms, lurching from place to place, leaving bodies in his wake, all of it without so much as a line on a map to follow.

Everything—survival, freedom, even ending it all, if that's what he decided to do—depended on timing, on having a plan and seeing it through, even if that plan was no more specific than what parking lot he would be sleeping in and which city he was headed toward next.

He had to get back on tour. It was the only place where he could make some kind of life, where he could be what he was now without giving up entirely what he had worked so hard to become after the change.

He opened the door and stepped outside. It was warm, with a light breeze that carried smells of livestock and manure. Cows. So this was West Virginia.

The tingling had started in his fingers by now. It had been two days. Like clockwork. The cramps were just starting in his stomach, a thin line of hunger, a twist that he knew would become a throb and then what he could only think of as a paralysis. His mind had been locked on the pain, desperately and futilely searching for any way toward release, focusing just on the pain, the feeling of it growing and gaining purchase on his body, one cell at a time. All the while, his body had been moving, lurching, propelling itself forward toward that poor clerk. He was like a zombie, a dumb creature overtaken by hunger, its mind in one place while its body moved steadily toward whatever it could do to sate the hunger. He had been no more in charge of his body than a monarch flapping toward Mexico.

Not this time. He started toward the cornfields and followed the scent of the cows. This was what he would be eating if he was registered anyway, some combination of cow and synthetic human blood and whatever else they put in there to reduce—how did they did say it?—"biological urges or other socially inappropriate behaviors."

He followed the cornfield over a ridge and then he could see them, ten or fifteen cows standing along a small creek that ran from a stand of woods all the way up to a farmhouse that stood dark against the mountains. The house was maybe a half mile away and he could see no lights, could hear no noise, no other sounds of activity. He had learned to trust his senses and they gave him no pause other than the steady twist of the cramps in his stomach, the tingle that was moving up his forearms, as if he'd hit his funny bone and it simply wouldn't stop.

The cows stood, flicked their eyes back and forth, hustled away from the creek as he made his approach. He was, he remembered again, an animal, a hunter. There was a place for them in a natural ecosystem, some said, although in order for it to make sense, you had to take humans out of the top rung. In order for it to make sense, you had to imagine a world where humans, or at least traditional ethics, didn't really exist at all.

The pain twisted in his gut and started to throb up his spine. Again, he felt as if his body was taking over, moving quickly now toward an ancient cow with black and white markings, a huge gut that nearly scraped on the ground as she struggled to follow the rest of the herd. They were making noise now and a light went on in the farmhouse. Cain's body stopped the cow with a bite, and he let go while the warm blood exploded into his mouth, while he felt every cell retreat, control come back into his brain. A gunshot went off and he sucked harder. He heard a motor start up, let the cow drop onto the ground with a *thunk*, and slipped into the forest. He registered the movement of his body, quiet and efficient, the satisfying feeling of vaulting over logs and between trees, making his way through the woods and then doubling back toward the van. He was vaguely aware of not thinking, the freedom of his mind momentarily turning itself off, allowing instinct to take over.

He neared the place where he had parked. He slowed. Noise. He crept closer, his mind awakening from whatever had happened when he had taken flight. Active meditation? Instinct?

He wanted to think about this more but there was no time. A three-wheeler was sputtering behind the van, its headlight illuminating the license plate. A man, older, with a baseball hat, sweatpants, and mud boots, was writing in a notebook, his head moving back and forth between the paper and the license plate. Cain walked quietly, but quickly. The man was muttering to himself, tucking the notebook into his breast pocket. He smelled of smoke and whiskey. Cain bit into his neck and yanked him off the three-wheeler. They landed on the ground and he drank.

Chapter 19

July 3, 1995. Noblesville, IN. Deer Creek Amphitheater.

The first thing he registered was the heat. It was hot. Way too hot. He was sticky, sweaty. Need to turn the heat down, he thought. Open some windows. He had to go to the bathroom. He would relieve his bladder, start the coffee maker, turn down the heat, and hit the bed for another hour or so of sleep. He wondered what time it was. A few short months ago, he thought, he would be heading to Special Readings, listening to Padma talk about her latest date or the new ridiculous thing her sister had said.

He listened for the chapel bells, the scrape and mutter of students moving toward eight o' clock classes. Outside, he heard birds chirping, car doors opening, groggy small talk. Car doors? He opened his eyes. A row of skeletons dancing in a line stared back at him, each of them doffing a top hat, holding a cane out to the side. They were close, too close. A few feet away. He turned onto his side and realized that he was sleeping in a van or a camper, in a makeshift loft. He smelled smoke and coffee. Marijuana.

He was at the Grateful Dead concert. Indiana. He was an undercover agent for the Department of Defense: Invasive Species Division. School was a long way away.

He remembered the girls, hanging out with them before the show, then the long migration into the concert itself. Inside, it was much like outside, a self-regulating free zone where laws seemed to no longer apply, where bikers and grizzled hippies shared pipes or pills or cotton candy with teenagers and middle-aged guys alike, where children toddled among passed out fraternity boys and groups of young ladies in billowing hippie dresses gathered near the exits to spin like dust devils along with the chugging, psychedelic country music.

The girl, Sunny, had promised to be his tour guide. "Your Julie McCoy," she said, referencing a show he hadn't seen for years, as she packed a bowl in broad daylight soon after settling up for his extra tickets. Nutter had been right. The tickets were all he needed to make his way in this world—they served as a reference, introduction, and legal tender. He thought about the envelope full of tickets locked in his glove compartment: Deer Creek, Riverport Amphitheatre, Soldier Field. Four tickets to each show, plus his new salary and the per diem he would never be able to spend out here on the road, and he was in pretty good shape.

He felt something on his crotch, something pushing up under the mattress, slowly. He realized how badly he had to go to the bathroom. But where was the bathroom? And what had happened last night after the show? Whatever was pushing up from the mattress pushed again, quicker this time, a bump up and down.

They had met up with some of Sunny's friends—older people, dirtier, people who looked like they'd been on tour for at least the duration of this one, and some of them, maybe, for years. They had hung out, drinking beers, the rest of them smoking cigarettes, Pete accepting the occasional joint or bowl, something Nutter had told him he would absolutely have to do if he was going to pass as even a marginal Deadhead. And then he'd done something they'd told him to never do under any circumstances: he'd taken a pill.

He was drunk. High. But that wasn't all. He knew, even this morning, that he was possibly still tripping on whatever he'd swallowed. His training told him it could have been anything from cat tranquilizer to pure acid to sugar pills, or anything in between. He took that pill not because he was weak or wasted. He'd taken it because finally, for once in his life, for the first time he could remember, he actually felt like he fit in.

The foot pushed again at his crotch, bounced him up and down twice, and he leaned over. On the bottom bunk, the girl, Sunny, smiled back at him. "Good morning, sleepy," she said. "You ready to go and get that stuff?"

Chapter 20

July 4, 1995. Outside Terra Haute, IN.

They were at a rest stop. Where, Pete had no idea. Somewhere off Route 70. He accepted the girl's offer of a toothbrush—fresh in the wrapper, produced from the glove compartment—and followed her toward the bathrooms. It was morning, but not very early. Around them, a few other Deadheads were stirring, meandering toward the bathrooms or sneaking into the woods. By the dog walk area, a couple changed a baby on a beach blanket, two small pugs wrestling nearby, identifiable as Deadhead dogs only by their tie-dyed bandanas. In the middle of the heads, normal people—families and truckers, men and women in suits and ties—bustled in and out, got their business done, bought a soda or grabbed a map, and hustled back to their cars. Pete had finished early and was waiting for the girl, Sunny, looking at a map of the state of Indiana.

"Yeah," she said, putting a hand on his shoulder. "We're in Indiana. That was a thing you were asking a lot last night."

"Indiana," he said. "I don't think I've ever been to Indiana before."

"Mentioned that, too," she said, a tease in her voice.

"I…" he started, but wasn't quite sure what to say. "What exactly…"

She let out a belly laugh. "Yeah, I was waiting for that," she said.

"I don't usually…" he said.

Another belly laugh. A woman with three small children lifted sunglasses off her eyes and glared, but Sunny didn't seem to notice.

"You were pretty fucked up," she said.

The woman gasped, covered the ears of the youngest child. "Some people," she said, and hustled the family back out toward the parking lot.

"You didn't notice that?" Pete said. He felt out of place in his tie-dye and necklaces. He wanted a shower, a cup of coffee, the *Washington Post*, and a cinnamon Pop-Tart.

"That bitch? How could I not notice that, man?" the girl said. She traced the map from "you are here" east, her finger trailing back toward Ohio. "I notice when people say things like that," she said. "But I'm trying not to care. You know?"

Pete nodded. He watched a young guy, only a few years older than him, walk out of the bathroom tightening his tie. I'm at work, he reminded himself. I have a job. A really well-paying, important job. That guy, suit and tie guy, is probably selling some kind of pharmaceuticals, office supplies. I'm in the front lines of the war on…what did they call it…invasive species.

"You know?" the girl said. "You told me you were a gentleman last night. Certainly acted like you were concerned for my fragile chastity."

His mind was blank. "What?" he said.

"Everybody was so fucked up," she said. "I still can't believe they cancelled a show. That, like, never ever happens."

"Did you hear anything about why?" Pete said. "I mean, I heard about some crazy stuff…"

"Gate crashers," she said. "They sent out a letter. Don't you remember reading that last night? 'This Darkness Got to Give,' it said."

Pete looked at the map. They were a long way from Chandler University, a long way from everything he had known.

"This darkness got to give," he said.

"A little dramatic but I get it," Sunny said. She fumbled in her purse. "From that one song, you know? New speedway or whatever." She slid a dollar into the snack machine, punched some numbers, and a cinnamon Pop-Tart fell with a *thunk*. She handed it to him. "Let's get going," she said.

"Where are we going?" Pete said. He opened the Pop-Tart, handed one to her, took a bite of the other. There were not many things better than the first bite of a cinnamon Pop-Tart and he realized with a jolt that he was starving.

"We're going to make that deal," she said. "Unless you got cold feet?"

"Deal?" he said. He was wondering how many Pop-Tarts they had in that machine, if it would look crazy if he bought them all.

"Your tickets for my friend's doses," she said. "Wow. You really were fucked-up last night, weren't you?"

Chapter 21

Jenkins waved his badge at the guard—another kid, but this one with a military bearing that he could tell was real—and gave him Tibor's name. "How long you expect to be in there, sir?" the guard said. He tapped something into his computer.

"An hour. Maybe just a half hour," Jenkins said.

"It true he used to be a cop?" the guard said.

Jenkins searched his face, but there was nothing there but one professional asking a question of another. "Yeah," he said. "My partner, for a while there."

The guard nodded, and Jenkins could see him mentally checking some box. So the stories about the old guy in unit 8B were true? He pressed a button and the gate opened.

The door was sitting open when Jenkins got to the apartment, the guard outside looking left to right with what Jenkins knew was precision and purpose. Training. "You Jenkins?" he said.

Jenkins held out his badge and a twenty. "Take a walk?" he said.

"I'll have to remain outside, sir," the guard said. He was short and stocky, with a nose that had been broken at least once and an eyebrow that formed a single line across his head.

"Just two pros talking," Jenkins said. "I know you'll stay outside but it…it doesn't feel quite right to me."

"Recognized," the guard said, "but I'm not authorized to leave visitors alone with residents."

Jenkins gave him his cop look, the one that cut through the bullshit. It was a look he'd perfected under Tibor's guidance and one that he knew saved him hours, maybe days, worth of time each year. It was a look that said, "We both know this is bullshit, so let's get to it and move on with our lives."

The guard stood his ground silently, and Jenkins pocketed the twenty, went inside. The old man was back in his chair, his blanket over his legs, the *Washington Post* crossword sitting on the side table. The case files were spread out on the dining room table, each victim in a row, chronological order. He'd placed a line of coffee mugs between the last few and those that had preceded them.

"You were right," Tibor said. "These last few, they don't connect. Something happened."

"He's sick. I think he…she…whatever. Something is wrong with it."

"It. Fuck you," Tibor said, but he kept his attention on the table. He took a sip of tea. "We don't get sick," he said.

"Never?" Jenkins said. "Ever?" He used the tone he hadn't employed for years, the one that asked for the inside scoop. It was the reason the feds had paired him up with Tibor to begin with—to catch a predator, you had to understand the predator, and nobody understood either side better than a ninety-five-year-old vampire who used to be a cop.

Tibor took his tea and sat down. He glanced over the crossword. Jenkins noticed the smell in the apartment—clean, antiseptic, a little medicinal. It smelled more like a hospital in there than it didn't.

"Nobody ever got sick. Ever?" Jenkins said. He had heard stories, like a lot of young cops who were paired at the time, government experiments in the sixties, strains of sickness from the old country that were still around and could lead to aberrant behavior. They had been briefed, secretly, although he never had much faith in the government in that way, its ability to keep its collective mouth shut about anything. They had given him warnings about spotting signs of…what did they call it…"existential exhaustion in your partner."

"Why don't you come out with it?" Tibor said.

"I heard some stories."

Tibor met his eyes. This was a trick, Jenkins knew, from dog training. The dominant dog will maintain eye contact. The submissive dog blinks. A hell of a lot easier to be the alpha, he thought, when you don't have to physically blink, when you're not technically alive. "Oh, Jesus Christ, Tibby," he said, "I know you're not going to blink. Why don't you just…"

"There were stories. You're right," Tibor said, his voice just above a whisper, his old-world accent peeking through. It was his natural speaking voice, Jenkins knew, and he almost never let anybody else hear it. Too much like those movie vampires. "An experiment. In the sixties when, well, you know. There were experiments. Not such an unusual thing."

"Experiments with what?" Jenkins said. He had only heard this much. That something had been done in some lab in California, that it had roots in the rest of the counterculture, best intentions, yadda, yadda, yadda.

"Acid."

"Acid? LSD?"

"It was a different time," Tibor said.

"But I thought," Jenkins said, "drugs didn't affect you people?" Jenkins' mind was reeling. This was the piece of the puzzle. It was starting to make sense.

"I've been upgraded to person. Thank you so much," Tibor said. He got up and walked slowly to the bedroom.

"I know you don't need to use the john," Jenkins said. "All four years together I never seen you so much as spit." He watched the man's back move through the door, heard a closet slide open, things being moved around. He walked to the window and looked out.

The parking lot was dark, fluorescent lights turned as low as they could get. A few loose residents wandered toward the fences. An old habit, he guessed, a phantom limb. They stared out at the highway or up toward the moon, meandered this way and that, like drugged rats in some test maze. A car came in through security and he watched each of them slink into a separate shadow, disappearing for all intents and purposes. He didn't know if this was some remnant of a different time—a hunter's instinct toward camouflage—or a kind of embarrassment about their current situation. Most of them, he knew, were too drugged to comprehend much beyond the minute by minute circumstances of their situation: pills, walls, Plasmatrol Extra, daylight retreat and nighttime wandering.

More rustling in the bedroom. Boxes falling, items being placed on the floor. "You okay?" Jenkins shouted. "I'm not going to have to come in there and use my superhuman strength, am I?" An old joke, never very funny. For some reason, Jenkins always slipped right back into the old patterns when he saw Tibor.

"Here's what I was looking for," Tibor said. He handed Jenkins a folder. Jenkins opened and a clutch of old black and white photos fell out. They were grainy, yellowed. He picked up the first one and smelled it—libraries, attics, industrial solvent.

"Sometimes you people..." Tibor said. He shook his head and sat back down in his chair.

Jenkins thumbed through the photos. They showed some kind of research facility—men in lab coats moving among a group of patients who sat in hospital beds behind a kind of chain link fence. Each of them was strapped to the bed, an IV coming out of their arms. Above the beds were additional fluorescent lights, single banks like a football stadium. It looked like the maximum-security ward at a hospital for criminals.

"The fuck?" he said.

Tibor mumbled and walked to the window.

Jenkins looked at another photograph, a close-up of a patient clawing at his cage. The photo was washed out with the fluorescent lights. The patient's fangs were drawn and he was chewing on the metal bars, a look of pure anguish on his face. His hands were shaking so fast they made two blurry mitts on the photo.

Jenkins turned to Tibor.

"What the fuck is this?" he said.

"Look closer," said Tibor.

Jenkins regarded the photograph. There was something about the patient. Something familiar. "This isn't..." he said.

"My origin story," Tibor said. "As I understand it, every superhero must have one."

"Jesus Christ," Jenkins said. The person in the photograph was in so much pain. The hunger on his face so plain that he wasn't a person anymore, had crossed over into something else, the centuries of civilization and culture tossed aside like a winter coat in the summertime. He looked closer. It was clear that this was a picture of Tibor.

"You said this thing was sick," Tibor said. "A sick animal."

Jenkins nodded. Words were not available.

"So am I," Tibor said.

Chapter 22

July 5, 1995. Maryland Heights, MO. Riverport Amphitheatre.

Something was gnawing at Pete the entire ride. He had only been on the job a week and still he had a feeling like he was doing something wrong. But his job was, as they had said, to become part of the scene. To hang out and learn who is who on tour, who might have information about the dead junkies. He wasn't supposed to arrest anybody, and when he'd asked about badges or guns or whether it was okay to get high on the job, to have a few beers, sleep in, generally live the life of a touring Deadhead, all Nutter had done was laugh.

"I said become part of the scene," he said. "No way you can do that without doing all of the above." Pete had just stared. This was the United States government? "You won't be drug tested, that's for damn sure," Nutter had said. "Least not in the way you're thinking." Pete picked at his cuticles, pretended to be examining his notes. "Not by us is what I mean," Nutter said. "You sure as shooting won't be drug tested by us."

Pete tried to put his worries at ease. He *was* becoming part of the scene. Just a few days and he'd made these contacts—Sunny and Rainey and Easy—had slept in a van and gotten high in the morning, smoked cigarettes for the first time, drank beer most of the time in between. He felt tired and worn out and couldn't have been happier. They had made a drug deal—two tickets for Pittsburgh for a baggie full of something that looked like dried worms. "Mushrooms," Sunny had explained. How much more a part of the scene could you get than that? Surely they would be happy with his progress so far.

He kept on forgetting to ask the questions—did you hear anything about these junkies dying? You ever meet anybody on tour who didn't, you know, seem to really fit in very well? He realized now, just two days in, how awkward those questions were, how the only way to actually stand out would be to start asking questions just like these. The whole deal seemed to be accepting people on face value. The only thing you *didn't* do was ask follow-up questions, pry into people's lives, the people and things they'd left behind to be standing out in a dusty parking lot, smoking a bowl and drinking beer and waiting until the gates opened.

In the forty-eight hours they'd spent together, he'd never heard Sunny mutter a bad word about anybody, with the slight exception of Rainey, her sister, and even then, nothing but jokey remarks about how big Rainey's feet were, or the "random" nature of Rainey's hair. In any case, he hadn't heard anybody worry over any dead junkies or notice anything that seemed out of place in any way, other than the calls of "five up!" that followed undercover police throughout the parking lot, or the occasional bad trip or low-level drug rip-off.

Right now, Sunny was making some necklaces while Rainey went out to meet somebody named "James Brown" who Pete assumed was not the Godfather of Soul, but he had also seen enough that at this point, he wasn't ruling anything out. Pete leaned back in his chair and took a drink of his orange juice. The parking lot was filling up. The sickness crawled back into his stomach. Diarrhea. This was not the best place for this to happen. He wasn't sure whether it was the beer or the way he'd been eating or the doubt that edged around the back of his mind whenever he thought about what he'd actually been doing for the past few days. He'd slipped into this world effortlessly, traded a few tickets for access to something he'd never before even considered. It had been as easy as Alice slipping down the rabbit hole. Too easy. And he liked it too much. The reason he'd been hired in the first place, he assumed, was because he was so unlikely to go all Heart of Darkness and really start living the life.

Or maybe it was something else. They certainly knew everything there was to know about him, more than anybody he'd ever met. More, in some areas—like his parents, their college lives, how they'd met and married and what they'd done until the day of the accident—than Pete knew himself. It was more than a little unsettling, but he wrote it off as Big Brother and government surveillance and tried to put it out of his mind, be happy that he had new information to add to the little stockpile of narrative he'd been able to cobble out of newspapers and what the social services people had told him.

Still, they had selected him. And now here he was, two days into it, and if he wasn't careful, he could wind up slipping into the current of this thing and never coming out. His stomach turned again. There were certain things, certain parts of this life that he knew were not well suited for him. The sleeping. The dirt. He craved a shower, some quiet, order in general. He thought about his apartment, a mere three hours away—so quiet and neat. The town would be deserted—one of his favorite times of the year.

.. He felt the tightening in his bowels. Need to get to a porta-potty. He'd avoided them his entire life, and now it felt like he was spending half his day waiting in line, trying to get the idea of exactly what was happening out of his head.

"Be right back," he said.

Sunny nodded. "Bring back a Dr. Pepper if you see one?" she said. "None of that Mr. Pibb bullshit."

Had he gotten himself into a domestic situation already, he wondered. They hadn't even kissed, but he felt a kinship toward her. And she was pretty, even here, without showers or makeup or whatever else it was that women did to make themselves attractive. "One Dr. Pepper, coming up," he said.

He knew by now to head away from the stadium, to the row of porta-potties furthest from the crowd. "The tourists," as Sunny called them. He walked past the now-familiar sights—T-shirt vendors, nitrous oxide tanks, vans that looked like they'd been on tour since Ken Kesey and the Merry Pranksters first hired the Dead to play the Electric Kool-Aid Acid Tests. He passed a kid who couldn't have been more than twelve selling soda for a dollar a can, made a mental note to get Sunny's Dr. Pepper on the way back.

Finally, he could see the row of blue porta-potties. No lines. He'd forgotten to bring along tissues, though, so he had to hope for some toilet paper. Stupid.

"Hey!" A middle-aged hippie with a baseball cap on backwards and a Jerry Garcia shirt was nodding at him.

"No thanks, man. I'm good," he said.

"Pete," the guy said. Pete stopped in his tracks. The guy nodded, something in his eyes changed. "Come on over here," he said. "Let's talk."

He stopped in his tracks. "How did you…"

The guy just held his hands up, his mouth pulled into a sarcastic smile. On second glance, there were a few things about the guy that didn't quite hold up. He was chubby, a typical middle-aged beer gut pushing the T-shirt up to expose a few inches of pink-white skin. He was wearing tennis sneakers—too new, unscuffed, the kind that might be appropriate on a boat or a country club patio, but not here, where sandals and Chuck Taylors were the clear footwear of choice.

Of course, Pete thought, he was one of them. Or, one of us. He looked back to where he'd come, but there was nobody looking for him, nobody he knew. Just the steady line of people selling things, others walking around, little clumps of people forming to smoke whatever it was they had to smoke. It seemed normal. It had been a long two days.

Behind the guy, Pete could see a woven blanket with a half-hearted assortment of bracelets and necklaces. "Come on," the guy said. "Take a look at my wares. Let's us have a talk." There was a trace of a New York accent. He turned around and walked over to a few folding chairs set up on either side of the blanket. He picked up a necklace and held it up as if he was showing it off, patted the chair next to him, and sat down.

Pete followed, but remained standing. "So, who are you?" he whispered. He looked toward the parking lot again.

"You've had a hell of a few days, huh?" the guy said. He was smiling, but there was no mirth in his voice. "Enjoying yourself, I see."

Pete felt the familiar déjà vu settle in. It was as if he was shrinking, like he was three years old again and hearing that terrible news for the first time. His breath shortened. Air cut off. He heard the sounds of gulping, wheezing, before he realized he was even doing it. He felt himself sit down on the ground. The feeling of dirt on his arms, rocks under his ass, his glasses steaming up.

"Hey," the guy whispered. "Hey! You're gonna blow both of us out of the water here, we have to call a fucking ambulance."

All Pete could hear was the heavy suck of his own breath. His lungs burned. Only that feeling—the burning, the wheezing. Not enough air. He imagined himself back on the steps of Glatfelter Hall. Fall day. Just a nip of winter in the air. He watched students walking back and forth, felt the slippery marble on his hands.

"Okay," the guy said, his voice faraway but insistent. "Okay, Peter. Calm down. Breathe." His tone had changed to the overly calm, mannered tones of a pilot making a routine announcement. In the back of his mind, Pete registered the word "professional."

The burning was dissipating, his lungs filling with air. He opened his eyes and the man reached out a hand. "Get in the fucking chair and let's work this out," he said.

Pete grasped his hand and was moving. The guy was surprisingly strong, guided him expertly into the folding chair. He reached into a cooler and held out a can of orange juice.

"No," Pete said, his voice scratchy and raw. "I'm good."

"You are not good," the guy said.

"I don't like," Pete said. His voice was coming back. "The can."

The guy dropped the can in Pete's lap. "Drink the fucking juice," he said. He put the necklace he'd been holding back onto the ragged blanket, picked up two bracelets.

Pete opened the juice and took a sip, then a gulp. He hadn't realized how thirsty he was.

"That was a hell of a way to make a first impression," the guy whispered.

Pete finished the orange juice and set the can down on the ground.

"I can't let these go for that!" the guy shouted suddenly, waving the bracelets around. He smiled at somebody behind Pete. "Guy wants two for one. I tell him, you find anything nicer than these around here and they're free. Best bracelets on the lot." Pete turned around to see two girls about his age, both with flowing patterned dresses and bare feet. "You guys want some bracelets?" the guy shouted. His tone was all off—more used car salesman than hippie craft maker. The taller girl gave him the peace sign and moved along.

"So they didn't tell you about me, brother, but here I am," the guy said. He let the bracelets drop and reached in his pocket. "You can call me Spot." He nodded his head with finality.

"Spot?" Pete said.

"That's my tour name. That's the only name you need to know. Now here's your first performance review," he said. "It's good you been doing what you're doing, but those girls aren't the people you're looking for." He reached into his cooler and opened up a beer, held one out to Pete.

"No thanks," Pete said.

"It's different here on tour, huh?" Spot said. He opened the beer and took a long drink. "Ahhh, but you don't even know. Pretty plum fucking first assignment, you ask me."

"So the girls?" Pete said.

"I got a wife. Two kids. A mortgage and a lawn to mow." He took another pull from his bottle. "I could get used to this shit."

"So I need to look for this…this person." Pete realized he wasn't sure what this guy knew. Nutter had been very clear about keeping his mouth shut about exactly what he was doing, even with local law enforcement, even with other federal agencies. Only Invasive Species could know exactly who he was, why he was out here. "I need to get out there more?"

"The girls you're with?" Spot said. "A good start. Important to have a tribe, as they say," he waved his hand around to indicate the parking lot. "A home base. Somebody to show you around, introduce you to somebody else." He took another deep drink from the can. "So what you need to do, my friend," he said. "Is start getting introduced."

"To who?" Pete said.

"Well that's the magic fucking question, isn't it?" Spot said. "Hey! I got those bracelets you been looking for!" he shouted at a group of guys walking by.

"Looking for the bathroom, man," somebody said, and they passed by.

"Well," Spot said, waving at the parking lot and the sad collection of jewelry in front of him, "we got work to do, so you best be getting along, little partner."

"Wait," Pete said. "How will I find you again?"

"Oh, don't worry about that, partner," Spot said. He pointed to the row of porta-potties. "I'm a forty-five-year-old man drinking beer all day long. You find the pissers, I won't be far away."

Pete turned toward the bathrooms. A long line now snaked along the porta-potties.

"One second, brother," Spot said. He held out a bracelet and Pete waved him off. "No, man. Don't think you understand," he said. "This one isn't optional." Pete accepted the bracelet—thick, black, woven leather, an off-white stone with a yin-yang etched into it at the center.

"What do I do with it?" Pete said.

"Just wear it, brother," Spot said. "And I should be able to find you if it comes to that."

Pete examined the yin-yang. "What?" he said.

"Tax dollars at work, my friend," Spot said. "Your tax dollars at work."

* * *

Sunny was sitting on a dusty Mexican blanket, setting up an array of bracelets on a makeshift stand made up of a few branches and some duct tape. Next to her was an open cooler of Heineken and a sign that read, "one dollar."

"More bracelets," Pete said as he sat down next to her.

"More?" Sunny said. She handed him a Heineken. "Hey, where's my Dr. Pepper?" She punched him in the shoulder.

"Shit, sorry," he said. "I can…" It had been less than an hour and he had totally forgotten. He wondered if his brain cells were going already, and then wondered why the idea didn't fill him with dread. Was he already too far gone?

She reached over and patted him on the arm and then squeezed. "Dude," was all she said, but there was warmth in her voice and he understood completely.

He sat back and regarded Sunny's makeshift store. The bracelets were a step up from the ones Spot had been pretending to sell, but still, he couldn't really imagine anybody pausing to consider them, much less make a purchase. The beer made more sense. "Where did you get those?" he asked.

"Bracelets? Traded some tapes, figured maybe I can make a few bucks so you won't have to…"

"I don't mind," Pete said. He stopped at telling her that he was getting paid to be here, getting a per diem on top of it, and that he was unlikely to ever go over no matter how many grilled cheeses, imported beers, joints and bracelets and vegetarian burritos they bought on Shakedown. He realized in a rush that he would never be able to tell her the truth about any of it.

"Hey, where'd you get that?" she asked, pointing to the new bracelet. She put a finger on the white stone, pressed at the yin-yang. "That's pretty nice."

Pete wondered if she was accidentally calling headquarters, whoever and whatever that might be. He yanked his hand away and stood up, trying to appear casual as he searched the meandering crowd for Spot or Nutter or a SWAT team. Nothing.

"Somebody needs to chill," Sunny said. She laughed and stared at him and shook her head but again, there was no anger in any of it and Pete was embarrassed to be so relieved.

He sat down. "Sorry. It's just...nothing. I'm not used to people grabbing me like that."

She held up her hands. "No offense, man. No offense."

"I'm not used to..." he started, but there were so many endings to that sentence that he didn't even know where he would start. "I got it from some guy near the bathroom. Just thought it looked kind of cool and the yin-yang was my mother's favorite symbol, I think, so..."

"That's awesome," Sunny said. "That's nice. Your mother. She sounds cool."

It was an invitation. Pete's face reddened. He had no idea why he had told this lie and it felt somehow like a validation and a betrayal all at once.

She stood and took his hands in hers. She looked him in the eye and he looked away. "It's okay," she said. "Hey. Whatever it is. It's okay."

He nodded and looked away. He felt the lump forming in his throat. It was the kindest thing anybody had done for him in how long?

She put her arms around him and hugged. He let himself be drawn in, breathed in her smell—apples and patchouli and smoke and sweat. He wondered how long he would be thinking about this moment. Remember this, he thought.

"Be who you are," she whispered.

He pulled back. "You don't...you shouldn't..." he started. He shook his head. He would never be able to tell her the truth. He searched the crowd for any signs that the bracelet had sent out some kind of signal. Could all of this even be real? He felt a tingling in his fingers. On the periphery of the crowd up ahead something caught his attention.

"It's okay," Sunny said, pulling back. There was a catch in her voice that he couldn't place, not anger or disappointment but a kind of familiarity and resignation.

There were things he didn't know about her, too, things he would probably never find out. She picked up the makeshift bracelet display and waved it around with fake gusto, as if she was trying to convince herself that she was moving on, that what she really wanted to do was sell bracelets.

In the crowd up ahead, one person stood out, an older man walking slowly toward them with a lopsided smile on his face. The man was short and seemed very out of place, dressed for casual Friday at the office instead of a show. He regarded Pete with open interest, like a scientist looking at a specimen. Pete flashed on an image of the man in a lab coat, his neutral features twisted into a grimace. There was a slight trembling in his legs and his feet felt like they were digging into the gravel. He tried to move as the man got closer but he found himself stationary, rooted into the ground like a statue.

Pete looked around, expecting to find a crowd gathering, but of course everybody went about their business.

"Bracelets!" Sunny said. "Heinekens one dollar!"

As the man got closer, he kept his eyes on Pete. He smiled and nodded. Pete tried to move but he was frozen. He jammed his fluttering hands into his pockets. In his head, a high sound, like static electricity.

"One dollar," Sunny sang. She twirled in a circle, already losing interest in her makeshift wares.

The man continued until he was a few feet away. He nodded at Pete, businesslike, his eyes conveying some message Pete understood as dominance, an alpha dog asserting its place in the order. The man veered toward Sunny and Pete tried again to break whatever spell held him frozen. As the man moved on past them, Pete felt himself pushed backward. He staggered.

"Dude," Sunny said. Pete lifted one leg and then the other. The whistling drained from his head. "Did you see that?" Sunny said. "It was like they just popped out of my hand."

Pete tested his fingers, his feet, his legs and arms. Everything was okay. But everything was not okay. He had come into contact with something. He was on one side and this man was clearly on another. This is why they had sent him here.

What else had Spot said? Start getting introduced.

"You okay?" Sunny asked.

"You know where we can find anything a little stronger than shrooms?" Pete asked.

"Dude, it was just some bracelets," she said.

"Not because of that," he said. "You know that."

Sunny looked at him strangely. "Do I?" she asked. She seemed to be making some calculation and he watched her eyes flicker with disappointment and then again resignation. "Sure," she said. "Let me pack up and we'll go see the man."

Chapter 23

July 5, 1995. Washington, DC.

"It's sick," Jenkins said. He thought of Tibor in his self-imposed exile. A better cop than every person in the room, and he was no doubt sitting in his chair right now, working through the crossword, his detective's brain wasting away in four walls of government security, reinforced steel, and a team of specially trained U.S. Marines ready to deal with any tenant who changed his or her mind about the arrangement. "*He* is sick, I mean," he corrected. He looked to the corner, where Associate Deputy Director Liddington stood at attention. Nobody could know he'd been to see Tibor. Nobody could know he had actually left files with the old man. "I mean, we have profiling that indicates this is likely a male," he said.

He moved over to the laptop and clicked to the next screen, a comparison of the first fourteen victims and the past two, the junkies' data bumped up against the citizens. He looked at the beginning and then the end. The difference was stark: the first two in the series were clinical, careful, bodies drained from two puncture holes in the side of the neck, laid down on the opposite side as if they had passed out or were resting, not so much as a broken branch or footprint on the crime scene. The last two were destroyed, huge holes torn in the neck and chest region, as if the thing that attacked them simply couldn't get at their insides, their blood, fast enough.

He looked at the ten or so officers in front of him, sitting at little desks like schoolchildren, munching donuts and drinking coffee like cops in some situation comedy. Crabtree was picking at his cuticles, staring at a spot just to the left of the three-ring binder Jenkins had prepared for every member of the task force. Jenkins was pretty sure the sports page was folded into a tiny square on Crabtree's desk, open, no doubt, to some article about the latest machinations of the Redskins. He considering calling on his partner like some vengeful second-grade teacher, but he would need Crabtree eventually and right now, when so much was unknown, when they were just dipping their toes into the work, was just not the time.

He advanced the slide again and the screen held just one image, a hotel clerk's broken and torn body lying on a cheap linoleum floor. "He's sick," Jenkins said. "And he's getting worse."

"How do you know?" Liddington asked. "My experience, these things are unpredictable. Like wild dogs, you think you have one that's trained but you can only train so much out of them."

"Aren't those werewolves?" Crabtree said. He made his jokey face, expectant and ready for a backslap or a high five.

"No, those aren't fucking werewolves," Liddington said. Crabtree recoiled as if he'd been struck.

"Of course, sir," he said. "Was making a…"

"Because fucking werewolves don't fucking exist," Liddington said.

Crabtree shook his head. Jenkins stared out the window. Here we go, he thought.

"What we have here is bad enough," Liddington said. "But it's explainable. Evolution is responsible for these creatures, same way it's responsible for the duck-billed platypus or the polar bear…." He paused and Jenkins knew he was considering whether he should go into his full diatribe on this topic. They had all heard it before. Jenkins didn't know if he could listen to it again, not so soon after seeing Tibor. It was bad enough that they'd been broken up, that the whole program had been dissolved, but that was as much Tibor's fault as management's.

Liddington caught himself, nodded to Jenkins, and turned for the door. "You all keep on going here. I want this shit stopped before it does any more damage. Before I have reporters knocking down my door." He turned and clicked toward the exit, then paused in the doorway and faced the room. "And werewolves don't goddamn exist," he said.

Jenkins waited until he no longer heard the sharp click echoing down the hallway. He looked to the room. Nobody cared. Crabtree was picking at his teeth, the rest of them stared vacantly at their notebooks or the screen and the bloody remains of the hotel clerk.

Jenkins advanced the slide again. "I'm sorry about that," he said, waving toward the screen. "That poor citizen was in the wrong place at the wrong time. Our job is to make sure that doesn't happen to anybody else."

The next slide was a chart, an illustration of the duration between attacks. "This is pretty simple," Jenkins said, warming to the task, his mind clicking this data back into place. "You can see when this starts, the attacks are three days apart, then two, then lately, one a day."

He regarded the room. Most of them were starting at their shoes, doodling, looking out the window. Crabtree got up and waddled toward the exit. "Too much coffee, Boss," he said. "Be right back."

"So as you can see, we're looking at one attack a day, past three days," Jenkins said. "We have men out at the concert tonight, law enforcement ready to scramble, to get in touch with us as soon as they see something that might match this pattern."

"What if there are more than one?" It was Robertson, a young agent out of Long Island.

"What?" Jenkins said.

"These attacks, they're all up and down the coast, right? Far west as Detroit? Far east as DC?"

"Yeah."

"So how do we know it's not a few of them?"

"There's a signature, the puncture mark is ninety percent unique. Not a guarantee that this isn't more than one, but put that together with the fact that it follows the Grateful Dead tour pretty much exactly, until we get to our friend the hotel clerk, along with that signature puncture, and we're pretty sure it's one guy, following the tour."

"But why?"

"That's what I was saying. They don't usually do this, obviously. This one seems like it's sick. It seems like it can't help itself."

Robertson snorted. "Can't help itself?"

"The progression of the data I'm looking at would seem to indicate an increasing loss of control."

"The fuck does that mean?"

"Like I said when I started," Jenkins said. "It's sick."

"So that is what I'm doing in here on a Sunday instead of watching the Redskins? What do we do with that?"

Jenkins knew Robertson was challenging him but he couldn't withhold his enthusiasm. Finally the data was showing them the way, or at least opening a door. "Where do you want to be when you're sick?" he asked.

"I don't know. Home?" Robertson said.

"Exactly," Jenkins said.

"So?"

"So we're going back on tour."

* * *

Jenkins looked at himself in the mirror. He adjusted the floppy hat, pulled the patchwork pants up and then down. He yanked at the sleeves of the decimated T-shirt. It was too small, and the pants were too big. He felt naked without his watch. In the hallway, he could hear people talking, and his first impulse was to sneak out the back door.

He turned sideways, took a few steps, dipping his head like Richard Pryor. But that wasn't right. How did they walk again? Like normal people. He took two steps back toward the wall, turned, gave his image in the mirror the thumbs-up. The thumbs-up? He had no idea what kind of greetings Deadheads used, but he was pretty sure it was not the thumbs-up.

There was no way he could pull this off if he didn't even know if they still did the thumbs-up or not.

He regarded himself in the mirror again. He looked like a federal agent dressed up like a hippie.

From the bathroom, whistling. Crabtree getting into character with "Touch of Gray," the only song he knew. Jenkins had been trying, listening to the cassettes he'd found in the evidence room. That particular part of the room was a wealth of source material—bootlegs and label-issued cassettes, CDs, T-shirts, and various paraphernalia that he imagined was used to ingest drugs of one sort or another. He liked the one cassette, *Workingman's Dead*. It wasn't much different from the country he listened to the in the car or the folk-rock Kathleen had pushed on him when they were dating. It was lazy country-rock, the lyrics obscure folk tales about trains and music and wolves that seemed like they could have been written in any era, could have sprung up out of the ground like oak trees or dandelions.

"Just a touch of gray, I don't know who dah dah dah…" Crabtree was singing. He looked completely at ease in his cutoff jean shorts and tie-dyed tank top, his hippie sandals and mandalas jangling on his chest while he swayed rather convincingly back and forth. "Just a touch of a gray, la da da da da da da daaaaa…" he sang.

Jenkins tried bouncing his head to the beat. It felt all wrong and he knew he was trying too hard. He'd seen enough of them to know they weren't trying at all, that the entire point was a kind of state at which you didn't have to try, you just swayed in the breeze, blown every which way by the music or the drugs or all of the above.

He imagined it helped if you were high.

Crabtree was bouncing around the room convincingly. To be blessed with no self-awareness, Jenkins thought, would be such a blessing. The late-afternoon sun was dipping beneath the buildings, breathing a glow onto the parking lot. Soon the old man would be here, if all went well. He wondered about telling Crabtree.

Anybody else, he would have sat them down already, explained exactly what he was doing and why, walked through contingencies and plans A through F. But he knew that Crabtree would just nod, chew his gum, put this latest failing in whatever place he kept his list of Jenkins' downfalls, and get ready for work.

"These sandals?" Crabtree said. He sprinted to the back of the room and then back to the front, stopped on a dime. "Pretty fucking good sandals," he said. "I might need to find a, like, less hippie version of these things."

Jenkins adjusted his own boots, tightened the wraparound laces that wound up to just under his knees.

"I don't know about this," he said.

"Come on, man," Crabtree said. He swung his head from side to side, moved his arms like a dancing robot. It was, Jenkins had to admit, a very good imitation of how the Deadheads danced.

Maybe I should just send him, Jenkins thought. Then he pictured what that actually might look like, Crabtree holed up in a VW van with some eighteen-year-old and a cooler full of Coors. Crabtree knocking heads and arresting some hippie for selling nitrous, or soda, or grilled cheese or beers. Leaving him out there with no backup, sending the body in without the head—it was not a good idea.

"How do I look?" Jenkins asked.

"Like a Deadhead."

He regarded himself in the mirror. He looked like he was dressing for Halloween as a cop trying to impersonate a Deadhead.

"I don't think that's true," he said. "But this is about as good as it's going to get."

Crabtree was packing his bag, putting his gun and beeper into a canvas fanny pack.

The two had never met, Jenkins realized, and they really couldn't have been any more different: the old country vampire and the gum-chewing linebacker.

"Hey," he said. "There's something I gotta tell you."

"Oh, Jesus," Crabtree said. "What now?" His expression was somewhere between affectionate and truly concerned, and Jenkins was struck again at how young he was.

"We're going to pick up some backup for the trip," he said.

"Uniforms?" Crabtree said. "Plenty of them walking around anyway, right?"

"No uniforms," Jenkins said. "An old friend. Partner."

Crabtree stopped cold, looked at Jenkins as if he was seeing something for the first time.

"That guy?" he said.

So he did know. Of course he would know. Of course before they put him on this assignment, they would have told him to watch out, step careful, report back if...

"Yeah." Jenkins said. "That guy."

Chapter 24

Cain wasn't sure if he was even going into the show, but he checked his watch anyway. They would be at least a few songs into the first set. He wondered what the first song was. They had been playing "Hell in a Bucket" a lot. He always hoped for "Iko Iko."

What the hell am I doing? he thought. There are much bigger things to be worried about.

There was everything to be worried about.

He pulled into the stadium—no traffic this late at night—and found a spot near the back of the lot, closer to the highway than he would have liked. He knew how the lot assembled itself, though, with the true heads arriving earliest, setting up their vans or cars or buses in the central spaces, near Shakedown or, if available, in the fringes down close to a river or some woods, the edges of whatever surrounded that particular stadium. A quick exit was not a priority: nobody was making a quick exit. Access to food and drink and drugs, proximity to the rest of the touring heads, and natural cover? Those were the priorities. Cain regarded the cars surrounding him. In-state plates. Hangtags. A dancing skeleton there, a dancing bear there.

He sat behind the wheel. Should he even think about going in? In his pocket, his ticket, wallet, and the baggie full of doses. He closed his eyes, tried to let himself go blank. But no, he couldn't feel the Dealer anywhere, couldn't feel anything other than the pull of the show and the slight embarrassment that he would be back here, despite everything.

It had rained and the parking lot glistened. The streetlights were hazy. As he walked toward the stadium, he could hear the dull thump of the band starting a new song, drums and bass coming together, guitars noodling their way toward a cohesive melody. What was that song? He kept his eyes on the stadium and picked up his pace. He passed the usual throng of kids and old hippies tending their wares—so serious they might as well have punched in—along with groups of frat boys pounding beers, teenagers changing a baby in the middle of the street.

It was beautiful. It was ridiculous and flawed and maddening. It was home.

How long had he been away? Two days.

Two days, two bodies. And one cow.

He had decided to get back onto tour and see if he could track down the Dealer. Certainly, there was something between them, some real and physical connection. Something more than physical, even.

He wondered about the doses again. They could be the answer. Or they could kill him once and for all, which would be, he realized, a different kind of answer. The worst-case scenario, the reason he hadn't so much as opened the Ziploc bag yet, was the simplest and most likely: that each dose would have the exact same effect as the original.

He had to find the Dealer.

The music was getting louder now and he recognized Bobby's gruff voice. The tune was familiar. A Dylan tune. "Desolation Row." He sped up.

Something hit his back and he stopped. Was that a bullet? He took a few more steps and something hit him again. Not a bullet. He put his hands up, unsure, really, why he was doing it, but expecting nevertheless to see a police officer, or a whole phalanx of them lined up with guns pointed. After what he'd done the past few days…

But instead it was the girl, tossing pretzels. She made a face at him, raised her eyebrows, and started walking away from the stadium. He followed her a few rows off Shakedown and into a little stand of trees. She looked around them carefully, and then hit him, hard, on the arm.

"Where the fuck have you been?" she said. "What have you been doing? I've been worried…" She stopped. "Just where the fuck have you been?" she said.

He wondered whether he could tell her. Certainly, she knew enough already, and hadn't, to his knowledge, betrayed his trust.

"I'm in trouble," he said.

She stared at him, then looked away. "Shit," she said.

For the first time since it had all began, Cain actually felt embarrassed. He'd been angry, sad, self-defeated, but now he actually felt himself blush, something he wasn't even sure was possible anymore. Perhaps, he thought, it was the ghost of a blush, like a phantom limb. He had read the science, understood, at least as much as he wanted to, the changes his body had been through. He knew his brain was still the same, was just reacting to the needs of the body. And now the needs of the body had changed even more.

There was something there, a clue to how this had all happened.

"What kind of trouble?" the girl said. Her voice sounded tiny. The question didn't sound like a question and Cain knew that she knew the answer. He looked at her and she looked away, pulled a beaten pack of Camels out of her back pocket and lit one with a Bic emblazoned with the AC/DC logo.

"Nice lighter," he said.

"You know how it is," she said. "You pick up whatever you pick up." She exhaled. "So what kind of trouble?" she asked.

"You don't know?"

"I have an idea but I haven't seen you for forty-eight hours, so no, I don't know exactly."

Her tone had changed. She had always been quiet, subservient, even. Cain looked at her. She was dressed in the camouflage shorts and a T-shirt with a picture of Tigger from Winnie the Pooh. Her hair was long and starting to tangle into loose dreadlocks. He wondered how long it had been since she'd bathed. Her feet were bare and calloused. He realized he could see her ribs. No track marks on her arms, and he'd never smelled drugs on her, but she was clearly really living out here, had been for some time. He reminded himself again: she had never led him astray.

"Why are you helping me?" he asked.

"I don't want to see this happen again," she said.

"Again?" he said.

"Shit. Look," she said. She glanced away and then met his eyes. "It's my job."

* * *

Cain had never let anybody in the van before. He squirmed behind the wheel, watching the girl settle in on the bench. She reached into her backpack and produced a small machine. She pushed a button and it whirred. "Piece of shit," she said, and set it aside.

"What's…" Cain started.

"So, where have you been lately?" she asked. "Sorry to be so blunt, but depending on the answer to that last question, and I'm pretty sure I know the answer, it's time for cards on the table."

"I've been…" How to explain it? He looked at her again. She seemed older in the interior light of the van. Of course, he'd only seen her in moonlight before. Now, he noticed the lines on her face. Because of the way she dressed, the way she acted, and where they were, he had pegged has as a college student. It was so hard to tell for him anymore, his reference points were all screwed up, being on tour and having no recent personal experience to compare it with.

The girl—woman?—picked up the machine and placed it her lap. She started typing. A computer, he thought. Small enough to fit into a backpack. No bigger, even, than a dictionary.

"You've been…" she regarded the screen. "Well, you've been on quite the little side trip, haven't you? Virginia, north into Maryland, west into Pennsylvania, where you make a little loop, and then wind up back here. If I were to—not that this machine could do it, mind you, piece of shit that it is—but if I were to, let's say, match this map up against unsolved homicides in the past three days…" She looked him right in the eye and he turned away. The doses were in the glove compartment. Tonight it would happen all over again. There were no cows in this parking lot.

"You know what my condition is," he said.

She nodded. "I do. But I don't know if I know everything."

"Neither do I," he said.

"That seems right, yeah. But still. I can't help you until I know what you know."

He thought about the Dealer. Something told him they would meet again tonight, a low frequency in his brain had started registering—a soft but steady blip-blip-blip that might as well be a map of the Dealer's own progress toward this very parking lot. "At this point," he said, "I'm ready to ask you to chain me in the open until morning so I can be rid of all this. So yeah I'll tell you what I know."

The woman sat up, clicked off the laptop.

"But first," Cain said, "there are a few things I need to know."

"I belong to an organization that is interested in monitoring and possibly resolving your situation," she said formally, as if reciting something from memory.

"What kind of…"

"Something between the government and not the government. We are…I guess you might say, 'off the books?' I don't have a card I can hand you. You can't talk to my supervisor or anybody, really, and if that laptop doesn't start fixing itself, neither can I."

Cain sensed that she was holding something back. She was giving him the official line, that was for sure. There was somebody who had given her these things to say, the computer she was so upset about, somebody out there who knew more than she did. In his head, the signal of the Dealer was getting stronger. Blip-blip-blip. "So your organization, then. What are you doing out here? How did you…"

He realized that she'd shown up a day, maybe two, after the Dealer, after Cain had taken his dose and sealed his fate. "Wait a minute," he said. "You're with them. With him. The Dealer."

"Dealer? I guess that is what you would think," she said. "He's much more than that. Much, much worse."

"And this is your boss?"

"Not anymore," she said. She leaned closer, put a hand out and he pulled back. "I don't think so, at least." She looked out at the people walking by the van. "Shit, I guess I'm kind of making it up as I go along," she said. "I'm not really happy with either side right now."

Cain was getting angry. She had known all along. He stood, knocked his head on the van's low ceiling, and sat back down. He shuffled out from behind the wheel where there was more room. He needed to move, to walk. He wondered if he could fly in this condition—angry, desperate. It was part of all the folklore, but he had never actually seen anybody go so far as to leap over a fencepost.

"I think you better calm down," she said. "Your heart doesn't pump blood anymore, but your body will still show the signs of human nervousness, of anger. Your adrenal glands still work."

Cain stopped his fiddling and looked at her. "You know things," he said.

"More than you, from what I can tell," she said. "But that's not unusual. Your kind. The lone-wolf type, I mean. You tend to move through life—your life now, after the change—without making any serious connections, which leaves you without much information at all about your condition. All you have is the movies and the books and whatever you pick up along the way, right?"

He nodded. There were others? He was a type?

"Probably didn't even know you still had adrenal glands, did you?"

He shook his head.

"But you can feel them. Right now. That feeling. It's adrenalin."

He opened his mouth to ask about the Dealer, if the blip-blip-blip that told him the Dealer was approaching was normal, if it was somehow adrenalin or heroin or something else the Dealer had put into him. He corrected himself: he had put whatever it was into himself, willfully and happily. He almost asked, but something told him to hold back. The girl had information—not just about the current condition, but about the condition in general. She hadn't yet mentioned the connection with the Dealer, the thing, whatever it was, that had held him shaking and frozen in place the last time their paths had crossed. It was still there, just below the surface, a physical presence like an itch. Closer-closer-closer.

"You're wondering what I know," the girl said. "If I'm hiding anything else. Whose side I'm on."

Cain nodded.

"I know more than you," she said. "There are things I can't tell you. It's just that simple."

"So why should I trust you?" he said.

"Because you don't have anybody else," she said.

Chapter 25

Cain slipped the doses into his pocket and followed the girl out into the parking lot. He thought about asking her if she knew what would happen if he took them, but then realized he didn't want to know the answer.

The parking lot lights crackled and popped. There were puddles where it had rained, the usual groups of people pulled into the usual circles, playing hacky sack or passing a joint around. They turned a corner and he could hear the hissing of nitrous tanks, could see lines of people snaking through the cars, waiting for a balloon or something heavier.

To their right, the parking lot receded to an older lot that was roped off from traffic. Long cracks were formed into the macadam, like fissures in a desert floor. A few kids threw a Frisbee in the distance. The sound of Bob Marley pulsed from the somewhere close—a live recording that he didn't recognize, "Trenchtown Rock" bouncing out across the abandoned lot.

The hissing got closer and they walked along the nitrous line. Kids, jumpy and inexperienced, bounced from foot to foot. This was one of the things he didn't like about the Dead's newfound success. "Touch of Gray" got some radio play and suddenly all kinds of people realized they could make a thousand percent markup on a cylinder of nitrous oxide and a dollar bag of balloons. It wasn't mind-expanding, had no history in the culture, the acid test or the Pranksters. It was straight dope—knock you on your ass and wipe your head clean stuff.

He felt the baggie in his pocket. Who was he to talk about expanding consciousness or not. He had chosen oblivion, even for just a brief moment, and now he was this caricature of himself, the human parts giving way to the animal nearly every day now. He didn't want it, but he had to admit that the past two times had been freeing. A release. He had spent so much of the past twenty-three years holding everything in, toeing the line, forcing himself to subsist on whatever he could scrounge, squirrels and rabbits and black market sheep's blood and out-of-date Plasmatrol. He had gotten used to living in the margins, forcing down that part of him that had emerged since the change, the part that was hungry and stronger than nearly everything else around, the part that smelled blood in the air and shit on the wind, that sensed when it was going to rain or, twice in Southern California, when the earth was going to move. He was like a swollen balloon, always pushing out, relying on the thinnest layer to contain everything that nature would have rise.

And the past few days had been different. He knew he had no choice and once it was clear that it was going to happen, he had simply given in, let it go, not so much enjoyed the ride as allowed momentum to pull him in a particular direction, had relaxed his defenses and permitted himself to be drawn into the undertow of the dose's desire. He needed blood, and he would have it. Giving in to this basic need was as simple as breathing, once he finally let it go.

Now, walking past the nitrous-eaters, staring at a greasy-headed kid in jeans and a button down accepting five-dollar bills, passing balloons off in exchange, Cain pictured himself leaping onto the moving van, not so much aiming himself at the boy's neck as allowing it to happen. The hot blood pouring down his throat as the smirk and everything else ran out of the nitrous seller. He would be doing the world, the scene, the Grateful Dead themselves a favor. Wouldn't he?

"Come on," the girl said. She pulled his arm.

He realized he'd stopped, was staring at the nitrous dealer, who had in turn read something in his eyes and was frozen in place, one hand reaching out for a five-dollar bill, the other holding a red balloon fat with the drug.

"The fuck are you doing?" the girl said. She tugged harder at his sleeve. Cain knew that he could do it. He could get away with it. The crowd would scatter. The police would be here soon. But soon enough? He could be in Ohio or West Virginia by the time they figured out what had happened.

He felt the baggie in his pocket. If he took a dose, would he have that feeling all the time? The lack of boundaries, giving in to what he really was all along. Who I really am, he thought. That was the key to figuring this all out. Be who I am. He felt the rise in his body, like adrenalin, like heroin, but better, more focused. He could feel like this all the time.

A tug on his sleeve and then *thunk*, a punch on his chest. "What. The. Fuck. Are. You. Doing?" the girl said. She pulled at his arm. The guy selling nitrous had gone back to handing out balloons and taking money. He glanced at Cain, turned quickly away, and put another five-dollar bill into the pocket of his shirt.

Cain took one step and then another. He heard the normal sounds of the parking lot—the nitrous hiss and the music blaring out of cheap speakers.

Behind a hedge, he saw a group of older Deadheads shooting heroin. Two men argued behind a T-shirt stand. Groups of high school kids roamed in baseball hats and collared shirts. He had felt it before, but he knew it now: there was an edge to the scene, something creeping. Three fans had been struck by lightning in DC. Even tonight, the gates had been crashed. Rumors that the band might actually have to cancel the rest of the tour. Maybe it was ending, he thought. Gate crashers and nitrous dealers and real criminals and kids who had never heard a song that wasn't on the radio or the television. Maybe it was okay if it was ending.

"Come on," the girl said. She was headed for the stadium. Cain took one last look at the nitrous dealer. The rise was still up in his system and he could hear the man jibber-jabbering away, making small talk, calling everybody "brah" or "captain," the disdain plain on his face. People like this didn't deserve to be here. If Cain needed to satisfy a craving tonight, he would know where to go.

He took a dose out of his pocket and dropped it on his tongue. Now, he thought, we will see what happens next.

Chapter 26

July 6, 1995. Maryland Heights, MO. Riverport Amphitheatre.

The guy they called Cassidy was standing in the middle of the bus, talking nonstop, gesturing and shouting and whispering and shifting seamlessly from one story to the next to the next to the next. He was trying as hard as he could, Pete knew, to approximate the real thing. To be Neal Cassady, inspiration and second lead in Kerouac's *On the Road*, driver of the bus Furthur for Ken Kesey and the Merry Pranksters. The original hipster. The original hippie. One of the reasons, maybe, some fifty thousand people found themselves in a parking lot in Pittsburgh in varying stages of drug-fueled euphoria, paranoia, or decline.

His training session had been brief, but they had shown Pete the movies, had made him read the books. "A person like you're going to be," Nutter had said, "would have read these books, would know these things. If you're going to be accessing the levels we're expecting, they are going to expect you to know your business and know it effortlessly."

Pete listened to Cassidy ranting and raving—something about his "old lady" in Santa Fe and a delivery of peyote via FedEx—and he wondered about the first part of what Nutter had said: "the person you're going to be."

Did they know? Could they have known he would slip so easily into the fabric of this thing he'd never even considered before? Was he so transparent that they could tell: this one will be getting high with dealers within two days of arriving on tour?

And if they could tell—if there was something in his DNA, his background, the permanent files on his parents that he knew existed but had never even seen— is that something they actually would have wanted?

He shook his head, tried to focus on Cassidy and the story he was telling. Now something about court, about a judge's ruling and a punchline about conjugal visits. Everybody laughed, smoke shooting up toward the roof like an engine steaming up a hill. He looked to Sunny and she rolled her eyes, held the peace sign out to him, and put her head on his arm.

Okay, he thought. Okay, that was not funny. I thought it wasn't funny and it was not. Okay. He focused on the steering wheel, black and worn on the sides. He stared at the insignia in the center: GMC. He breathed in and out, in and out. Cassidy had started up again and was feigning driving, turning an imaginary wheel to and fro, careening in his imaginary car over who knew where. I am high, Pete thought. Really high. This is okay. This is okay, okay, okay. We prepared for this. He flashed on his training sessions, he and Nutter in the hotel room with a bag of evidence. The man's soothing tones. Focus on an object. Breath in and out. In and out. Tell yourself you are fine. You have been through this. You have been trained.

He looked to Sunny and she was staring out the side of the bus. The show had started hours ago, and he could hear the tinny music echoing across the parking lot. A song they'd played last night, something about a guy and his uncle. In the end, the guy kills the uncle. He remembered because it had seemed so shocking at the time, and only to him. To kill a blood relative, and for what? But it was only a song.

"The person you're going to be." It was an interesting choice of words. He thought he had made his peace long ago with his situation, with being the only person in his family, nobody to look for or lean on, no template waiting to lead him forward into adulthood. But these past few days had been disorienting. Is this the person he was going to be? Sunny had said "be who you are." What was the difference between the two?

A joint was making its way toward him and he thought no, no, no. No, I do not want that. Sunny took a hit, held it in and coughed blue smoke up toward the ceiling. Pete followed its progress and watched as it pooled and then disappeared, seeping into the gray fabric like dew melting into a lake.

Cassidy waved at somebody walking by in the parking lot, then waved again, and then smiled. He stopped in mid-story and Pete told himself not to sigh audibly. He sighed anyway. Cassidy was halfway out the door, though, moving out to the parking lot where he immediately started up with an entirely different story. The guy was in character. You had to give him that.

Sunny handed Pete the joint and leaned over, put her head on his shoulder. She smelled like apples and pot and cigarettes and sweat. She smelled like Sunny. Again, he made a note to remember this and wondered how he could ever tell her the truth. He couldn't. "Gotta go back but I don't know if I can right now," she said. She yawned and closed her eyes.

Pete took a hit from the joint and adjusted himself so his back was firmly against the wall of the bus. Sunny breathed in and out, in and out, and he thought she might actually be asleep. He wondered if the joint had been laced with anything. That was certainly a possibility, one they'd covered in detail in his limited amount of training. He thought about trying to make himself throw up, but he knew it was too late.

Training. Now that he was out here, he realized how lousy his own training had been. If this is how the government trains agents, he thought, there's no wonder the world is in chaos.

They had said something about his schooling. Academic background. It hadn't made sense, necessarily. Had always kind of stuck in his craw. "Religious studies majors can have a certain…open-minded nature, in terms of the folklore," Nutter had said.

The folklore was what they called it. What they meant, of course, was something different.

He felt a tingling in his hands again. He looked at his right hand and then his left. They were jittering, almost buzzing. He stood, wobbled, stumbled out of the bus. "Wait," Sunny yelled. But he needed to protect her, get as far away from her as he could. The man, whoever he was, had known that they were together and it was clear that his earlier demonstration had been just that. Pete's legs were moving. It was crazy. He was no good at this job. He was super high. He was a federal agent. He was moving toward something, somebody. What and who, he had no idea, but he was moving.

Chapter 27

Cain followed the girl through the crowd and back up into the stadium. "New Speedway Boogie" was playing in the background, Garcia noodling through a set of runs somewhere between blues and funk. All around them, people made their way to and from the infield—hardcore Deadheads headed toward the stage, new fans and suburban kids headed toward the beer stands or the bathrooms.

She knew that he was tripping now, or that he'd taken a dose, at least. It didn't seem like anything was happening yet, but she had begun to regard him carefully, checking her watch every five or so minutes and then looking at his hands and his eyes to gauge…something.

They walked up the stadium stairs and into the first level, through a throng of Spinners ecstatically whirling as Micky and Billy started to pound out a slow march from "Space" into something that he couldn't quite recognize yet. His brain said Europe, early seventies. Vintage years. Europe had been easy. After the change, it was the first place he had felt even remotely at home, and the loosened restrictions on his kind had allowed him to finally make some peace with who he was now. The Europeans had lived for centuries with his kind, and there was a system in place, a market that existed apart from the law and the straight world. It was no harder to find blood in Europe than it had been to find weed or acid in San Francisco in the sixties.

Perhaps Europe was the place to go, after this was all over. It would be harder now—many things had gotten much harder. The band hadn't been to Europe since the eighties, and Cain had settled into the habit of simply following, had relaxed his will to the easy non-decision of going where the band went, staying where they stayed, and then heading off to the next city.

For the first time, he wondered if there was a next tour. This tour had gotten ugly—gate crashers and nitrous dealers. The crowd had changed. At first, he didn't want to believe it, had thought the complaints were just old heads unwilling to let go of the fact that the fan base was doing what it always did—churning out the old and welcoming in the new. But now, as his own transformation had taken place over the past few months, he could see it more clearly. Things were changing. There may not be another tour. Depending on what he had placed on his tongue roughly an hour ago, there may not be another show for him at all. That was the choice he had made, and he was almost surprised to realize that he was okay with it.

The girl nodded at him in a way that he was positive meant stay put, and walked into the women's room. Packs of kids roamed the yellow hallway. He smelled sweat and piss and popcorn and weed. Cigarettes and beer and something sharp and chemical.

He turned toward the source of the smell and saw him, leaning against a wall smoking a cigarette and drinking a soda from a straw. The Dealer.

Chapter 28

Jenkins stood in the beer line, at least twenty or thirty hippies deep, and watched the crowd. Crabtree had convinced him, maybe rightfully so, that the only way they could distinguish themselves from undercover cops was to go ahead and loosen up. Tibor had disapproved, he could tell, but these were different times and this was a different job than the one he had done with the old man. Most of the people in line were kids—trust-fund sophomores playing at being hippies. They were smoking, drinking, getting high right there in the bowels of the stadium. At the exit, a group of girls twirled in tight circles, like little tornadoes edging for the open space of the infield. Everything smelled like weed. He could have arrested maybe three-quarters of the crowd for one thing or another. But, he reminded himself, he was after bigger fish.

He watched a group of kids passing a joint around, standing no further than a few feet away from Crabtree. One of them tapped him on the shoulder and offered a hit. Crabtree accepted and took three hits in quick succession, turned to Jenkins and released a thick plume of smoke. He was fitting in a little too well, perhaps.

Jenkins flexed his knee. He wasn't used to standing around like this, not anymore. The flight had been quick, three hours to fill Tibor in on everything they knew, feed him all the data that was available. The old man had taken everything in, filing each detail, each murdered junkie, location, and date, into the computer of his ancient brain, and Jenkins had watched and marveled at the stores of information that must reside there. Centuries of weapons, injuries, motives, times of death, pieces of evidence. He pictured the old man's mind as a massive filing system stuffed full of notes, the paper growing ever thinner, more white, lined, manufactured, and sterile as the years went on and on.

For his part, the old man simply nodded, scribbled on his little note cards, constantly arranging them into piles, rearranging, adding cards and moving from one pile to the other. He had asked few questions, his uncharacteristic reticence, Jenkins knew, a nod to the presence of Crabtree. There was little in the folklore that the old man would support, but the idea that there was some sixth sense, that like dogs, they could tell if somebody was open minded, sympathetic or not, was something he had told Jenkins about early in the partnership.

More than once, when they had arrived at a crime scene, Tibor had opted to simply wander through the crowd, to turn off his senses and let what he called his "radar" take over.

That's what he was doing now, trolling around the stadium, waiting for something to register. Where he actually was, Jenkins had no idea. "Wandering?" Crabtree had said, watching the old man wade into the crowd and fade away, like a fish let off a hook. "You had to sign five waivers to get him out of that place, take him across state lines, and you're just going to let the guy fucking walk around and…check shit out?"

"It's not like that," Jenkins had said, but when pressed to explain exactly what it was like, he realized he was actually unable to provide any further detail.

The line was taking forever, each of these kids rolling out with four or five or six gigantic beers, heading toward the lawn with big stoned smiles on their faces. Jenkins scanned the crowd, his mind registering data, data, data but none of it any good. A kid smoking a joint here. A hippie spinning in an acid daze there. None of it was going to help them find the guy. None of it was going to save anybody's life tonight.

What were they even looking for? Somebody out of the scene. Of it but not in it. Somebody who was sober, if the folklore was to be believed. That was a start, he realized, but the place to collect that data was not in the beer line. Fucking Crabtree.

He played with the walkie-talkie in his pocket. It was still. No buzzing, no messages. The plan was flawed, had been all along. There was, he had to admit, not really much of a plan at all, other than three grown men walking around in tie-dyes, one of them waiting for "radar" to kick in, the other two fighting the urge to arrest nearly every single person they came into contact with. Best case scenario, they stumble upon something. Worst case, Tibor had himself locked up in that facility for a reason and they have two, maybe more bodies to deal with by the end of the night.

And now they'd taken themselves to the one place in the entire goddamn stadium their suspect was certain to avoid. Unless, of course, he was stupid enough to be doing the same thing as they were—trying too hard to fit in, fitting in all too well, accomplishing nothing.

He wasn't stupid, Jenkins knew. Not this one. But he was sick. Of this, Jenkins was sure. It was the only way to explain the aberrant behavior. Sickness, or a death wish, and if he really had a death wish, there sure as hell were easier ways to carry that out.

No, he was sick, and like a dog that can't stop eating weeds, their guy needed blood, real blood, not Plasmatrol or pig's blood or whatever they were selling on the black market wherever the tour happened to land him. He needed real blood, and he needed it immediately.

He looked over at Crabtree, who was spinning with the girls in the exits, his eyes closed, barefoot, a smile on his face like Jenkins had never seen before— pure joy, like a baby, like the only thing happening in the world right now was the drumbeat pushing out from the stadium and Crabtree's own stupid sandaled feet spinning, spinning, spinning.

Holy shit, Jenkins thought, maybe their perpetrator actually liked the Grateful Dead. Maybe he was a Deadhead before he had gone through the change. They had spent so much time tracking the shows, trying to find a geographic nexus where the guy might be living. They had studied maps and highways and traffic patterns, as if they were tracing the path of flotsam through a series of rivers. But that wasn't it at all. He wasn't floating. He lived here. This, the kids in line and the music and the parking lot and the cars and vans and buses, the whole damn thing: this was his home.

Chapter 29

Cain wiggled his fingers. They were working just fine. So far. He wanted to send some kind of signal to the Dealer, but he wasn't sure what he would say. Back off? Hi there? More? What? Instead, he just stood there, watching the guy sip his drink, watching him nod and then slowly walk away. Watching him stop and gesture, once, crooking a finger in the direction of the parking lot, grimacing impatiently, like a father waiting for a dimwitted child to figure out how to tie his shoes.

He followed. Why was he following? His first impulse was to go get the girl, but then he realized that she was at his side, one hand behind his back, silently guiding him, moving him along, keeping him on track like a guardrail.

The Dealer walked through the tunnel of the stadium, past one exit and then the next and then the next, past masses of people waiting for the bathroom or the beer stand or the popcorn. Whirling groups of Spinners twisted in the light of each exit, the sounds of the band playing "Box of Rain" pushing out through the openings. Cain caught a glimpse of the stage and then the back of the stage and then the infield. They were walking in a circle. Cain told himself to run, to feed, to grab the girl and hold her hostage. He should be in the van right now, heading south, or north, or anywhere but here. He never should have taken that first dose. Without it, he would be standing on the infield right now, not just among the crowd but in it, a part of it, as much as his condition would allow. He would be swaying back and forth, his own particular version of the Dead dance that was now being practiced to varying degrees of success in every foot of the stadium. Now, what was he doing? He was following a dealer in a circle around the stadium. He had left two bodies behind in in the past two days. He had killed more, fed more on live humans in the past few weeks than he had in the entire previous time since the change.

He couldn't help feeling like the dose had transformed him back somehow. His soul. As a vampire, he had lived a virtuous life, as much as the condition would allow. And now, after the dose, he had reverted back to the soulless, selfish way he'd lived as a man. He realized all that he had lost in the past few months—his entire way of being in the world had been careful, cultivated, thoughtful. And now he was…what? An animal. An animal who killed in cold blood and not only gave in to his most base desires, but enjoyed the release of those moments, longed for it when the grip was not upon him and he again labored under the restrictions of responsibility.

"Where are we going?" he said again.

"Just keep walking," the girl said. "We're being followed."

"Followed by who? The police? Others…like me?"

"All of the above," she said, and pulled him along the concourse, following closely in the shallow wake of the Dealer.

Chapter 30

July 6, 1995. Maryland Heights, MO. Riverport Amphitheatre.

Pete could hear music trickling over from the stadium, the sounds of drums and spacey guitar. This is what people are talking about when they talk about noodling. He had only been on the job for less than a week but already "Drums/Space" was his least favorite part of the show. It was much better, he'd learned, high. It was much better on the infield, amid the whirling, dancing mob that would be shouting their delight now, tripping in circles, many of them tight in their own heads, the music perhaps the only connection between their own chemically-altered consciousness and those twirling or spinning or curling up on the ground only a few feet away.

He had reached the place, was sure of it. Whatever had been guiding him remained steady now. Something was approaching. But now what was he supposed to do? He waited.

Chapter 31

Jenkins followed Crabtree, walking as fast as they could without looking more conspicuous than they already were. They swooped along the clumps of Deadheads that gathered near the beer lines and the entrances, pushed past staggering hippies, slipped through spaces where groups of people danced in that ragged, loose-jointed shuffle that Jenkins knew he would never get close to mastering. It was easier moving through this crowd than others—they were malleable, in no hurry. They were stoned, and barely noticed the two poorly-disguised undercover agents currently pushing toward Concourse B, where Tibor had spotted...something.

"Concourse B. Now," was all he had said.

"What?" Jenkins had shouted into the walkie. But the old man did not respond.

They moved into another crowded area and Jenkins caught a glimpse of Tibor's black-gray hair receding quickly toward the exit. "This way!" he said.

As he ran, he kept Tibor's stately head in his sights: bobbing quickly with the old man's huge strides. As they grew closer, he could see Tibor's arm held out at the side, cordoning them behind him. "What?" Jenkins said.

"Three of them up there," Tibor said. One like me, a girl, and then..."

"Then what?" Crabtree said.

"A blast from the past," Tibor said.

"The fuck does that mean?" Crabtree said. He tried to step even with Tibor but couldn't get around his arm.

Tibor looked at Jenkins. "This is what we talked about before. The researcher. Portis. The one who..." There was a tone the Jenkins had never heard before. He was scared.

"I need to know what's going on!" Crabtree shouted.

Tibor stopped, turned around. "Ahead of us, on foot, is what I believe to be our perpetrator. He is being led by a young woman and they are both following a man who I believe to be a former scientist and enemy of the state, who compelled me to kill a citizen in Washington, DC seven years ago. The reason I am currently confined to a federal facility." The old-world accent had kicked in full force.

Tibor quickened his pace and then he was running. Jenkins followed, Crabtree close behind him. Jenkins felt for his service weapon, thought about taking it out, and then thought again. Best to wait until they were sure there was a situation. You could never tell what the security people would do when faced with a middle-aged man in a tie-dye waving a revolver around.

They neared an exit and then they were flying down levels, working their way to the parking lot. They exited and all of a sudden it was quiet, the concert a tinkling in the distance, the sounds of crickets and the occasional whine of nitrous tanks echoing across the lot, mixing with their own ragged breathing. Tibor slowed. "Drat," he said, his own voice even, his breathing regular.

Crabtree sucked in breath. He laughed and Jenkins remembered that he was still probably high, and maybe a little bit drunk as well. "I lost them," Tibor said.

Chapter 32

July 6, 1995. Maryland Heights, MO. Riverport Amphitheatre.

Cain followed the Dealer, the girl silently steering him, out into the parking lot and past the usual in-show scenes—kids gathered in circles, passing around bowls, vendors getting their wares ready for the post-show Shakedown, middle-aged men with short hair getting into cars, making their way back to the suburbs in time to get enough sleep for the morning. They moved past the old buses and the vans and the cars that had obviously been on tour for years, down a few rows and over to narrow path that went into the woods.

Funny, Cain thought, the idea that he could slip the woman's grip, make a break for the van and be on the way to New Orleans or Seattle or Mexico, had never even entered his mind.

His mind. He stopped to think of the concept. He felt…how to describe it. Not high, necessarily—this was not as much fun as he remembered being high or drunk to be. But still: altered somehow. It wasn't the all-consuming hunger-pain that gripped him now before a feeding, no burn in his head, no tingle in his fingers working outward to all his extremities. But still, not exactly in control, not like before. It was more like being on tracks, led gently but decisively in a certain direction, down a certain path. What he wondered about is what would happen when the tracks were removed: would he have any more control than he did when the pain took over his body and he was compelled to feed.

He wondered if he had ever had that control, or if all those years of careful living, of scrounging Plasmatrol and sheep's blood, watching the clock, planning several moves ahead, had all been nothing but folly, the same reckless Hell's Angel in different clothing, watching the clock until it was time to release the constraints once and for all.

The Dealer looked around. The girl's hand was still on Cain's arm. "What are you doing?" she said. "You agreed that…"

The Dealer closed his eyes. Something in him seemed to relax. "Soon," he said.

The girl released her grip and took a few more steps into the forest. She turned and regarded Cain and for the first time he saw real pity, real fear in her eyes.

They were in a low forest, just ten or fifteen feet away from the parking lot, a place where Deadheads would slip into the woods for a smoke or a deal or a bathroom break. The moon was full and he wondered about the folklore. He had never felt a pull, but had heard that he should, and now…but that certainly had more to do with the doses he'd taken than any celestial body.

Cain felt like he was underwater. His fingers began to tremble. It was coming back, but back with something else, some sleepwalking quality, like he was here and he wasn't here, like the leash had somehow extended to all his extremities, to everything. He could see the entire situation plain as day—the woods, the Dealer, the girl, the stadium lights behind them in the distance. He could hear the music, the shouts of Deadheads in the parking lot, the low rumble of cars starting up. The pain started in his neck and rolled steady up over his head until he felt like he needed to put holes in his temple to relieve the pressure.

The girl took out a dose and handed it to him. He didn't think, just put it on his tongue. He thought about all those nights in San Jose, doing just that in some bar or hotel room. Somebody would hand him a pill and he would swallow. They would bring in a girl and do what they would. They would hand him a gun, a knife, and he would use it.

"Almost here," the Dealer said. He took a few more steps into the woods. Cain felt something approaching from behind. He was so hungry. The pain would not stop. There was only one thing to be done.

He closed his eyes, tried to relax. It was going to happen.

Chapter 33

July 6, 1995. Maryland Heights, MO. Riverport Amphitheatre.

Pete heard them coming and slipped back into the woods. They were an odd group, a small, older man moving purposefully into the woods, followed by a large man with a biker's face and unblinking eyes being led by a girl who looked, although it certainly couldn't be her, remarkably like Padma.

The tingling in his hands increased. He felt a presence in his head, almost like a static, a thin connection to…something.

After the second group went charging past—two of them clearly undercover cops, the second an older gentleman dressed in strange clothing for a show, with an overcoat that went almost down to his ankles, dark black shirt and pants—Pete slipped along the wood's edge until he found another path leading parallel, and he crept along the trees until he could see the first group. The woman and the first man were backing up slowly, coming his way as their trails connected. The other one, the biker, was shaking, turning red, hitting himself in the head with balled fists and making guttural sounds. Pete wondered at first if he was going to turn into a werewolf. Then he saw the next group, the two cops and the old man, moving into the clearing.

It was all so fast. Too fast.

The biker grabbed the first cop and pulled him into the woods, the man's head wedged into the crook of one arm like a football. It was a wonder the guy's head didn't pop off, he thought, and then he heard the noises, the sounds like leather ripping, the screams and cries and gurgles, and he realized it would have been better if it had.

And then it was over and he could hear the tinkling of music coming from the stadium, the older cop swearing and calling for an ambulance on his walkie-talkie. These men were obviously police. The biker was a vampire, and dangerous. And what was the girl who looked like Padma doing there, and the other older man who looked like some kind of professor? He took a step back, and then another. There were sirens in the distance. He made his way slowly back toward the parking lot.

Chapter 34

"I don't understand," Jenkins said. He looked at Tibor, at the two scruffy, Deadhead-looking men on the other side of the table, and the one who refused to sit down, who stood at attention like a fed in a movie with his three-piece suit and fedora. His mind was still processing, spinning, struggling to put these new pieces of data into appropriate places. "I mean," he looked at Tibor. He knew he was transferring all his feelings about Crabtree, the guilt and the anger and something else that he didn't want to think about just yet, onto the old man. But still, he couldn't help it. He was pissed off. "Throw me a fucking bone here, man. "

Tibor was calm, measured, as always. "I had heard rumors. But I didn't know. Not for sure."

"We are a deep operation," the one who seemed to be in charge said. The other two, the Deadheads, nodded. "The fact that we're here in this room is due mainly to a field decision that I would not have approved. And of course, the terribly unfortunate circumstances behind Officer Crabtree's…"

He let whatever it was that had befallen Crabtree linger in the air. Jenkins fought the urge to shout, throw a chair across the room. He had watched hundreds of people in this situation and had always wondered at their anger, the primal need to assign blame, to start with whoever happened to be in the room at that particular time. He knew he was acting just like them, that everybody in the room knew as well. Still, a secret government agency tracking the vampires, working on the same case, with people inside the community? It would have been good to know. Maybe Crabtree would still be dead if they had known. But maybe not.

"I don't think it's his fault," Tibor said. Everybody turned.

"Really?" the older undercover agent said, the doubt thick in his tone. He was standing near the window, turning a pack of cigarettes over in his hand. This one really did look like a Deadhead, hard like the older ones seemed to get, like the constant touring, whatever kind of lifestyle they were leading, had sharpened up all their edges. "You would, though, wouldn't you?"

Tibor ignored him. He was writing on a legal pad. Jenkins had seen this before. "What the fuck is that supposed to mean?" Jenkins said. He knew what it meant, but he was ready for a fight. God, he thought, that would feel good. To just let everything out, turn off his editor for a moment and just give himself over to something physical. He hadn't punched somebody, been punched, since he'd been promoted to desk sergeant, since David had been born and he'd stopped going out to bars. It had been years and years and all of a sudden it felt too long.

"I know the man," Tibor said. "Portis. Doctor Everett Portis."

"What are you saying?" Jenkins said. He wanted to give Tibor an out, a way to go back to his quiet life.

"I know that man," Tibor said. "From a long time ago. The sixties. He is, or maybe he was, a researcher. A scientist out of Stanford. He was doing work with LSD, some other psychotropics, effects on the normal population, effects on those like us. The differences. The theory, as close as I could tell, was there was something in the differences, something that could provide some answers."

"And?" the older undercover guy asked. He put a cigarette behind his ear and sat down, his leg pumping. Jenkins wondered how long he'd been on the road.

"This is where it connects," Tibor said. "Maybe. One of the things he was working on was mind control. Combine the right psychotropics and the power of suggestion becomes more than that. That kind of thing. For our kind, there is something there, maybe. In the folklore it goes both ways: those who can control the mind, those who can be controlled. Again, I believe the theory was that there was something in the differences, something chemical that would allow him to…"

"To do what?" Jenkins asked.

"Control us all," Tibor said.

"Mind control? The vampire just said mind control," the undercover agent said. He put the cigarette in his mouth. "Can I smoke in here?" he asked.

"Outside," Jenkins said. It would be fine with me, he thought, if this guy never came back.

"Have you ever heard of Project MKUltra?" Tibor asked.

"Rings a bell," the undercover said.

"It was federal. CIA. They were researching mind control and one of the ways they thought it could be done was through LSD. They were giving it to hookers, to johns, scientists for some reason. People like me." He paused and looked around the room. "Had people jumping out of buildings. There were hearings in the seventies and they shut it down, destroyed almost all the records. It was bad."

"That's fucking insane," Jenkins said.

"There's a lot of fucking insane stuff out there," the undercover said. The other one was drifting over toward the windows. God, he was young. Jenkins had called for an inside man. Is this who they had sent?

"I caught a case," Tibor said. "A murder. The suspect had been, or was still, depending on who you talked to, a subject in one of Portis' studies. Funded by the government. MKUltra. The deceased had been a rival of Portis', some academic dustup that none of us understood. Seemed to me like they were arguing over nothing, words on a page, but, well, academics… Anyway, we had a lot of dots and couldn't make them connect, but most of them pointed back up. To the CIA. To MKUltra."

Jenkins thought about his own revelation. "It's sick," he said. "The vampire."

"Same as me," Tibor said. He looked at Jenkins and nodded. So it was all going to come out.

"I wish I knew what the fuck you guys were talking about," the undercover said.

"That's not the only time our paths crossed," Tibor said.

"Can we do some police work now?" the undercover asked. Jenkins balled his fists but kept them at his side.

"I was a subject in a test," Tibor said. "I thought maybe they could, I don't know, make me normal again, back to being just a person, just a cop. But Portis was up to something very different and I think he's still working on it."

Finally, Jenkins thought, a direction on this case, the pieces started to come together. He turned to Tibor. "If we find this guy, you think there's a chance we can find out how to, I don't know, reverse whatever he did to you?"

Tibor nodded. "I would be remiss if I didn't note," he said, "that there's also a chance that he could…"

"Yep," Jenkins cut him off before anybody could catch up. "There's a chance of anything. All the more reason to get back out there."

Chapter 35

They were moving, rolling, when Cain awoke. They were in a car. His compartment, whatever it was, was dark and close. He lay on his back. It was perfectly black, or almost so, a dark gray hovering over everything. He reached a hand out to feel the roof above him, the walls to the left and right. They were solid, covered in some kind of fabric. They were driving, could feel the bumps in the road, hear the traffic sounds mixing with low conversation behind his head.

He tried to remember how he had gotten here. The show. The Dealer and the girl, the feeling coming on in the middle of the woods and then…

He hoped the people in the clearing, the man he had killed, weren't cops, but knew in his gut that they were. Something in his brain had registered them even in the middle of everything that was happening. Something about their clothes, the way they ran, clutching walkie-talkies or badges or hidden service weapons. In his years with the Angels, the art of spotting a police officer had been a much-valued skill—second only, perhaps, to fighting or riding or dealing. Since the change, he had used that skill more than he would have guessed, although always to slip away silently, remove himself from a situation instead of starting one.

He almost laughed. There had been a time when his biggest problem was trying to maintain life as an unregistered. Now he needed to stop killing people. He was a cautionary tale, the exact situation the right-wingers would trot out to make the case that integration hadn't worked, that his kind needed to be put away, locked up in a place where there was no such thing as unregistered. They would ensure that for his kind there would be no such thing as the open road, or another show next week, or any of the careful but free life he'd been living for the past twenty years.

The vehicle, whatever it was, slowed and stopped, made a right turn, and then slowed again. Wherever they were, there were stoplights and traffic. He was in a bus or a truck. A big one.

He wondered if they were at Soldier Field. It was likely there or some criminal facility, a federal prison devoted to those like him.

He had snapped the guy's neck. A cop. Not his first cop, but the first since he had made the change. The first since he had really, consciously tried to change the way he lived. The first since the night at the motel in San Jose, maybe the worst undercover he'd ever encountered. He had snapped the man's neck the minute they laid out the drugs, the rest of them with no idea that the guy was even a cop, Cain so sure he hadn't wanted to waste a second once he figured out the cop was alone, didn't want to risk a name or a voice out on a wire somewhere. They had another room and another scene in another town, so he snapped the guy's neck and they put their shit back into the backpack and they moved along to the next town and the cops were none the wiser. Not until way later. Not until he had already undergone the change.

He heard voices. He didn't know how, but he knew it was night. He was, after all, awake. He was alive. For now.

There were two options. Either he was with the girl and the little nerdy-looking guy, the Dealer. Or he was with the feds. He wasn't sure which would be better. The feds at least were transparent, easy to understand, to place him in some continuum that made sense in a larger context. The girl and the Dealer were more complicated.

The two of them were an odd pair, hard to figure. Cain remembered what he could from the night before: the cops, the hunger overtaking him, worse than it had ever been, a hard ache in the center of his head that throbbed like an ocean current. This was a part of him now, something he could tamp down but could never put out completely. He could cover it up, drown it, feed it with blood, but it would still be there.

He heard people knocking around, low voices in the vehicle. He couldn't pick up the words but their tones were serious, scared even. Voices rose and he picked up a word or two, his own name and the phrase "scientific responsibility." He wondered what that meant, but he knew it wasn't good, could tell by the tone of the voices that they were worried.

He felt for a door handle, a lock, some kind of opening. There was a rough patch in the smooth metal, what he assumed had been a kind of handle that had been sawed off, and he clawed his fingers at the place where the floor and the wall connected. If he could jam a finger, a fingernail in there, he could force the thing open and…what? Kill everybody inside? Fight his way out of whatever they were in? Fight his way to where, exactly?

A knock. "Remain calm." It was the Dealer's voice. So there was that, at least. They were more likely to be at Soldier, or in an isolated compound somewhere, than one of those mythical federal facilities. "I'm going to open the door now."

Cain shifted in the chamber, balled his fists. He posed his body for an attack. Then he remembered where he was, what he'd done. These people were the only ones who might be able to get whatever it was out of him the same way they'd put it in.

"It won't work if you try to come out fighting," the Dealer said. His tone was flat, almost amused. "You have noticed that I have the ability to…control is too strong a word. Influence your actions, yes?"

Cain knocked, once, on the partition closest to the voice.

"So it's really quite simple for you. Come out fighting and you'll force me to influence your actions. Come out like a gentleman and we can talk."

One dose, Cain thought. One moment of weakness in his carefully managed life and here he was with no choices at all.

"I won't kill you," the Dealer said. "If that's what you're deliberating about in there. I'm afraid it's not going to be that easy for any of us from here on out."

Cain's hands began to tremble again, just lightly, moth's wings flapping at a lantern in the dark. He flashed on a memory from his childhood, sitting around his grandparent's trailer with his cousins while a campfire burned.

"You may be noticing a shaking in your hands," the Dealer said. "Just a little demonstration."

Cain imagined tearing into the Dealer's neck and the trembling grew, butterflies into birds. He struggled to lift his arm, knocked once on the side of the container.

"Very well," the Dealer said, and immediately the tremors retreated. Retreat was the right word, Cain thought: whatever was in there was still there, but the Dealer had made it go away, if only for the time being. Cain thought about that helpless feeling, letting himself go and letting his body do what it wanted to do. He knew it could happen again at any time.

The side opened and Cain waited for a beat. He put a foot out first, then another, shimmied until he was out of the container and standing unsteadily in what seemed like a large bus. A tour bus? The Dealer was standing a few feet back, a syringe filled with clear liquid in his hand. The girl was behind him, fidgeting with her hair, near what looked like a communal area with low couches and a single table.

"Mr. Cain," the Dealer said. Behind him, the girl shook her head and scowled. She looked out the window. Cain could see the usual parking lot scene through the tinted glass. "Welcome to the last stop on this tour."

Chapter 36

Pete changed the channel. On the screen, a young woman stood in front of a jeering crowd. A woman with hair that didn't move and a fright mask of makeup held a microphone in front of her, asked "Do you really think we should believe you?" The crowd went crazy, shouting and shaking fists.

The young woman wagged a finger at them. "That's right! You know you waaaaaaant it!" she teased.

Pete giggled. He wondered if he was still stoned, even now. They had been here, in this station, for hours, the rest of them leaving him in this holding room. He considered whether he should be mad, or worried. He was, technically, a government agent, even if he'd only been one for a few weeks, and mostly what he'd done was follow the Dead around and ask not enough questions. Mostly he was tired.

He wondered what other people his age were doing. Sitting in offices, making spreadsheets, daydreaming through graduate school lectures. What was Padma doing? He always pictured her in some kind of romantic comedy situation, shopping with her sisters, walking along the streets of Manhattan laughing, all of them beautiful and free. She was his only real friend, and how much did he know about her, anyway? Not much. Nothing more, really, than what a real government agent could piece together in a few days of surveillance.

The girl at the show had looked a lot like Padma, but there was no way it could actually be her. It had all happened so fast.

The door opened and he sat up, wondered briefly if he had done a bad enough job to get fired, or even worse, be thrown in jail. Could they do that? He had no idea what they could do. The tall cop, the one who had been wearing the tie-dye, was standing in the doorway with a bag of chips and a coke.

"I'm Jenkins," he said. He handed Pete the chips and the soda.

Pete tried to talk and a squeak came out. He cleared his throat. Had it been that long since he'd last spoken? "Vandenberg," he said. He opened the chips. He hadn't realized how hungry he was, how thirsty. Maybe he was still stoned.

"That was my partner," Jenkins said. "Crabtree was his name." Pete nodded. He had no idea what to say in this situation. What could you possibly say? "He was a good man," Jenkins said. "He was a…he was… Ah, to tell you the truth he was kind of a goofball. You know? Kind of a fuck up. One of those guys you're not quite sure what he might do next. Kind of guy, though…" he swallowed, stood up and walked to the window. "The kind of guy you want on your team. *That* kind of fuck up."

Pete had no idea what this guy was talking about, what the good kinds of fuck ups might be. The emotion in his voice was clear, though, and Pete had seen him stomping around the crime scene, combing through evidence like a machine cutting through alfalfa.

"What I need from you," Jenkins said. He placed a hand on Pete's shoulder. He sighed, resigned to something that Pete knew he would never understand. "Is help."

Chapter 37

Jenkins walked toward the window and watched the kid squirm. Jesus. This is what it's come to? He barely looked old enough to drink. He clearly hadn't shaved or washed himself for at least a week. He stunk like weed and beer and dirt, a smell Jenkins knew he would forever associate with this brief, disastrous tenure as an undercover Deadhead.

Still, he had to give the kid credit: he was there. A week on tour, barely any training, and no prior connections, and the kid had been standing there when they got through the clearing. Somehow, he had done his job, found the one who was sick. He was there before Jenkins, before Crabtree, even before Tibor. Standing there in the clearing, far enough away to avoid trouble and close enough to know who was making it. Like a cop.

Jenkins thought about Crabtree lying there on the ground, the sound of his skin ripping, of that thing sucking his blood in gulps like a man gasping for air after holding his breath for too long. He knew he'd never forget that sound, all of it mixing together with Crabtree's own gasps, his throat struggling to draw air, the sound of a human engine sputtering out of gas.

The kid was watching the television again, his eyes widening as Jenny Jones' audience grew more raucous. He smiled a stoned smile. The smile of a kid who didn't know he was being watched. David hardly smiled like that anymore. He was too cool. Like the piggyback rides and Saturday morning trips to the diner, the cartoons and spelling tests and Hawaiian Punch, his innocent smile was just one more little-boy thing put away as he retreated further into his own teenage identity. It was good, Jenkins reminded himself. It was good. A boy needs to pull away at a certain age. He remembered something Tibor had told him earlier, wondered if it was true, if this kid met the criteria he'd heard about, which at the time had seemed way too specific.

"You an orphan?" he asked.

The kid jumped. His head turned and he seemed to be remembering where he was. Jenkins wondered how long the dope would stay in his system, or if he was always like this. "Parents were killed when I was little," he said. "Ward of the state."

"How long you been out of school?" Jenkins said.

"Not long," he said.

Jenkins realized that this was the extent of the kid's resume so far. His entire professional experience had been the past few days, culminating, of course, in the death of Crabtree, that ripping sound, the vampire gulping blood and Crabtree making that high animal whine.

"Wait," the kid said. "How did you know that?"

"Heard some talk at a party once. Or, I don't know, party after the party after the party. You know, police, even federal, they talk. They drink and then they talk."

The kid made eye contact and then looked away. "Your friend," he said. "Not the one who died. I'm sorry about that," he said it quickly, unused to this kind of conversation, Jenkins could tell. "Your other friend. The tall one. The one who walked off. Is he…"

Jenkins nodded. "Used to be my partner," he said, surprised that he was telling the kid this much, more than he had told the other undercover. "Back in the day there was a program, paired us up like a buddy comedy, Eddie Murphy and Nick Nolte, you know?"

"A pretty good movie," the kid said. He was still watching the television, toying with a bracelet on his wrist.

Jenkins wondered what David was doing right now. He had spent so much of the boy's life away, out, pacing around in rooms like this one, compiling data, searching for one person and then another. It would never end.

He should never have gone to lunch with Kathleen. Still, it was nice to see David in what was clearly becoming his natural element. Band practice. A girlfriend. He was smart enough to see the situation for what it was, to clear the hopeful blur out of his eyes. Chicago was David's home now. With Kathleen. He would get four visits a year, and then three, and then two. Maybe if he played it cool, went along and didn't make a fuss, David would look at some East Coast schools, maybe even American or George Washington. But somewhere along the line, sometime when Jenkins had been standing around a murder scene, or putting together bits of information until they started to form pieces, following Crabtree into a stash house or suspected affiliate's place of business, or maybe in small ways during all of those times, in increments over the past few years, he had lost David to Kathleen and Chicago and this was the boy's home now.

"So now?" the kid said.

Jenkins opened his notebook. "This is the part where you tell me everything you know."

Chapter 38

July 9, 1995. Chicago, IL. Soldier Field.

Tibor scanned the crowd. They were ragged, dirty as he and Ilya had been coming off the boats those many years ago. They were the same age, as well, most of them—late teens, early twenties, some older people mixed in, as clearly lost and doomed as the elderly had been at Ellis Island and then the Bronx. He remembered them as apparitions, the old country beamed into the New World, clothed in black wool and clutching their rosaries or crosses, their Bibles printed in Italian or Polish. They had stumbled along with the rest of them, herded like animals from one holding pen to another. They had made the journey, but it seemed impossible that they would actually live at the destination.

And now these new ghosts, the gnarled, bearded, wonder-eyed children of the sixties that had somehow, against all odds, remained alive and stumbling around the parking lot of Soldier Field. They clutched their version of rosaries—bongs or bowls or baggies full of powder, clumped into their own little groups like the Czechs or Hungarians fresh off the boat and already reeling in the New World.

He wondered how they were still alive. They were not careful people, and a lifetime of living carefully—two or three lifetimes if he was being honest with himself—had led him to distrust those who lived any other way. An overdose, an undercover cop, a heart attack, stab wound, infected cut, or mouth cancer—somehow, they had avoided all of the millions of things that may have ended their brief stumble through life. Through some combination of luck and pharmaceuticals and genes, they were here. They were wrinkled and too tan, skin and bones or obese, one-legged or blind or in perfect health, falling down drunk or stoned or tripping on who knew what, but they were here. Somehow, they were still here.

Tibor scratched his long sleeve tie-dye. He felt naked without the overcoat. It had been years, decades, since he'd been outside without it. The sun had just gone down and the parking lot was getting loud. Drums, recorded music, shouting, the steady hiss of nitrous oxide tanks emptying into balloons. It was all too much. He remembered that he'd checked himself into the facility for more reasons, really, than just the one. It was quiet. Regular. Orderly.

He had the kid in his peripheral vision. Sitting there. Just sitting there, drinking a beer, looking around like he was waiting for somebody. Was he waiting for somebody? The kid was raw, but there was no doubt he had something—instincts or luck. He had been standing in that clearing before the rest of them had gotten there, had avoided running right into the gauntlet like poor Crabtree. That ripping sound. Tibor had only heard it a few times before. Another reason for a careful life.

"Hey, man. Hey. Man." Tibor looked down. A small old man, his face grizzled but eyes shining that wonder-eyed hippie gleam, a combination of childlike and wise and tired and amused. "You need?" the guy said.

"Need," Tibor said.

The man backed up a step, held out his hands. "Don't want nooooo trouble, man," he said. "Specially with you all."

"You all?" Tibor said.

"You smell like a cop, man," the guy said, taking a few more steps back, looking for an escape route. "No offense."

Tibor nodded, continued to scan the parking lot as the man slipped through a row of cars and disappeared. The kid was still in place, still sitting there. He was drinking another beer now, smoking a cigarette. This was significantly different police work than Tibor had done in his day. He thought about that first year in the NYPD. 1922. Maybe not that different, after all.

He hadn't thought about those days for so long. Nostalgia served no purpose in a careful life. The best advice he had been given after going through the change had been to leave the old life behind. Ilya and Prague and those first few years on the force—careless, freewheeling days of lager and dancehalls, all of them seemingly equal parts thrilled and astonished to find themselves walking among the skyscrapers of New York City, and not just living but actually thriving in the New World—he had shed the memories like a cicada discarding the husk of its shell.

Ilya. He looked around at the women in the crowd, young girls in flowing skirts and long hair, dancing and laughing, rushing from one place to another. Things were so different now. Ilya would have loved it, would have thrived in the modern world. He hadn't allowed himself the extravagance of memory for so long and wondered why it would come to him now, here, in this place with these people who followed a rock and roll band from place to place. Ilya had never even heard

120

of rock and roll. He pictured her dancing in one of those halls, always a little faster, more loose than the others. Her hair flowed and there was that look in her eye like she was making fun of him and she wasn't. She was always so much smarter than him, always the smartest person in the room.

He paused, allowed the stream of people to pass him by. Four girls danced outside a station wagon and he watched them with awe. They were barefoot and whirling, laughing and singing. He allowed himself the memory of Ilya for a few moments more, pictured her here, by his side. He could practically feel the sweet weight of her arm on his back, the brush of her hair on his cheek. Her smell—the perfume she had insisted on buying even though they really couldn't afford any luxuries—came rushing into his nose and he gasped.

Ilya is not here, he told himself. They had made their decision together, seventy-three years ago, and it was the right one. He told himself that again now. It was the right decision. The life he was leading, the life to which he'd been condemned, it was no way to be, especially for somebody as alive as Ilya.

It wouldn't do. There was no point in nostalgia, no place for even the ghost of Ilya in his life now. He forced himself to open his eyes. He focused on his boots—black, leather, sitting here and now on this stretch of concrete. The walkie-talkie buzzed. He searched for a place where he could talk without being conspicuous. There was work to do.

Chapter 39

The Dealer had gone, left them alone for the first time. The girl fiddled with a magazine and then a file that was stuffed to bursting with printouts and official-looking reports. She looked different. Older. She had abandoned the ratty T-shirt for a solid button-up, the shorts replaced with jeans. Cain snuck a look at the folder. Printed in large block letters: "PROJECT MKULTRA: CONGRESSIONAL INQUIRY."

"Why were you helping me?" he asked. "Before, I mean."

"If you do anything, you know," she held up a syringe filled with clear liquid. "This isn't in the mythology, but it will kill you, sure enough. May be where the silver thing came from, some people think. Maybe not. There is dispute in the community."

"What community is that?" he asked. He wondered how quickly he could get to her, if she could get the syringe, or maybe her neck, before she had a chance to react. He realized that he didn't feel anything. Or, he felt normal. The ache was nowhere near the surface right now, buried, at least for the time being. Normal. It had been some time.

The girl looked at him and rolled her eyes, as if they'd had this same conversation many times and she was tired of it. She took off her glasses and cleaned them on her shirt. If I jumped right now, Cain thought, I could rip out her jugular before she got her glasses back on. But there was that feeling. Normal. "The scientific community," she said, as if the answer was as plain as day.

"The scientific community," Cain said, "has no interest in..." he hesitated to say the word, and then felt silly for it. He hadn't said it in all these years, had held off even, when possible, in his own head, as if the simple uttering of the word would somehow cement the whole situation. As if it there were options, some genie to shove back in a bottle, an exit strategy that involved something other than sun, silver, or stake.

"Vampires?" the girl said, and Cain flinched. The girl smiled. She put the syringe down and turned her attention to a stack of papers sitting on the driver's seat. "So interesting," she said. "So reluctant to even say the word."

"I…" Cain started.

"Don't worry," she said. "You're not the only one. Most. Rare is the vampire who is not afraid to say the word vampire."

"There are others?" Cain said. "I mean. I know there are others. Obviously. But you do, too? You've met…others?" It had been so long since he'd even had a conversation with somebody. He was out of practice, awkward at even the basics of personal interaction.

She stopped with the papers and turned her attention to Cain. She cocked her head. "Do I look like some kind of amateur?"

"You used to," he said. "You looked like, I don't know, everybody else around here. Which I suppose was the point."

He thought of the way she had helped him, practically teeing up those poor junkies. How many had it been? He tried to remember but just felt a bad taste in his mouth. He forced it out of his mind. No upside.

"Invasive species," she said.

"What?"

"What the government calls it. Calls you. Vampires. Department of Invasive Species."

"There's a department?" Cain wondered what else he didn't know. For the first time in a long time, he wondered if he should have tried to make some connections, find some community other than the band and the shows and the Deadheads. He had chosen to live among that community, but not to be in it. He lived on tour the way a burr lives on the coat of a dog. He had made his choices for a reason, but now he was realizing how much there was to know, or at least how much he didn't know.

"So what is this?" he asked. "What are you and him doing?"

She put the papers down and crossed her arms. "It was—it is, rather—an experiment."

He nodded.

"But you must know that already," she said. "And now we're at the end of the experiment."

"And how does it end?" he said.

"That," she said. "Is entirely up to you."

Chapter 40

They were walking toward the stadium when Pete felt it again, a tingle starting in his fingers and the back of his head. He stopped.

"What?" Jenkins said. "You getting it again?"

Pete nodded. He moved off to the side, away from the crowds that were stumbling or spinning or trudging toward the stadium. Soldier Field stood in front of them, looking solid and bright. "I think they're headed this way," he said.

"Who?"

Pete turned to Jenkins, who was making a signal to Spot, meandering along a few feet behind them and over a row in the parking lot. "I don't exactly know, like, how this works yet," Pete said. "My fingers are shaking, my head feels weird and I just kind of feel like one of them is coming this way, but other than that, I don't know."

Jenkins nodded. "Sorry," he said. "If that's what we have to work with then that's what we have to work with."

"I definitely feel like something is headed this way," Pete said. "Almost like it's…calling…or like there's some kind of connection we want to make. I'm not doing a good job of describing it but, I don't know, man."

"It's okay," Jenkins said.

"I mean, I really don't know what it is, even."

Jenkins put a hand on his shoulder and squeezed. Pete looked at his face, the lines around his eyes. His first partner was old enough to be his father, a thought he was surprised he hadn't had earlier. "Do you have any kids?" he said.

Jenkins smiled and nodded. "I do. A son. He's fifteen."

Pete nodded. He had no idea what to say next. He realized that he had very little experience talking to adults outside a classroom. The vibrations grew stronger.

There was a tightness in his head, a feeling like his body was preparing itself for something.

"Oh, hey," Jenkins said. "I'm really sorry. Talking about my family and you…" he drifted off.

Pete could see Spot off to the side, playing with a yo-yo. Somewhere in the parking lot, Bob Dylan was singing about being stuck outside of Mobile with the Memphis blues again. People wandered by, almost in slow motion. A kid of maybe ten or twelve walked by carrying a tray of Rice Krispies Treats and a warm smell pushed into Pete's nose. His mouth watered. He could see every translucent hair on the kid's arm. What was happening?

"Are you…is something…" Jenkins said. Pete nodded. Jenkins motioned to Spot, who palmed his yo-yo.

Pete wanted to speak, but he couldn't find the words. He took a step forward to see if he could do it, then another step back. He lifted his shaking arm and scratched at his cheek. He could still move, could still do whatever he wanted to do, even with whatever it was mounting in his body. Preparing. For what, he had no idea.

The feeling intensified and he put his hands in his pockets before somebody could notice the way they fluttered like bees. Jenkins was speaking into his hand. He would be calling the other vampire, Pete thought, the one they called Tibor.

He felt strong and alive and he was surprised to find that he was unafraid. Whatever was coming, he was ready for it. He turned to his left without thinking and knew that he would see them there soon, making their way through the crowd.

Chapter 41

Tibor had some idea of what he was running toward but not really. His senses had not been stirred at all on this day, and he did not know how to evaluate their failure. It had always been hit or miss, more a divining rod than a metal detector, but he had always felt something, a stir in a certain direction, and these past few explorations were the first time he'd come away with nothing at all. He took that piece of information and put it in the back of his mind. It would make sense later, he knew, when there were enough supporting details, enough scribbles of information to assemble a full picture.

He was moving the same way as traffic, weaving in and out of the strange masses lurching toward the sounds of drums just starting up in the distance. He did not understand these people. Blessed with the miracle of a normal human life, they had chosen to shackle themselves to...a musical group?

It simply made no sense. Music was fine, pleasant. Those early nights in the Bronx, before the change, he and Ilya had danced through midnight, losing themselves. But that was more about Ilya than the music. To attach such importance that you were following one particular group across the country, across decades? He had seen much come and go and felt like he understood most of what happened in the world. The one gift of the change had been time, the long view, the ability to notice as the world evolved. Given time, he could assemble the data, could see the picture as it became evident. But this, these Grateful Dead people, they were beyond reason.

He slowed to a brisk walk and looked for Jenkins and the boy. His fingers began to tingle. Tightness in his head. A feeling he hadn't felt for years, decades. He knew that Portis was near, could feel himself being drawn forward. He looked down at his legs, watched them churn. It was like he was outside his body, watching from above as he moved ever forward. A group of kids were kicking something back and forth in a small circle and Tibor registered that he would have to walk around them and was surprised when he bumped into the tallest one, knocking him to the ground.

"Dude!" somebody called after him.

He wanted to stop but he couldn't. He flashed to a hospital room, a younger version of Portis, a needle moving into his arm. He bumped into a group of young women twirling in a circle and kept moving. He had volunteered for the program on the assumption that the government wouldn't put its own agents in harm's way, but something had been off from the start. Portis was nervous, jumpy, and too quick to laughter. It was the sixties and half the world was stoned, but at that point he still believed that certain professions were above discretion. The rooms were dirty and disorganized, papers stacked in the corners, strange devices sitting around gathering dust. He was asked to sign a release form but Portis was unable to locate the papers and asked Tibor to sign an envelope in their place.

But still, he had done it. They said they were working on an antidote, that there was a slim chance his "symptoms," as they called it, could be reversed. A chance he could be buried next to Ilya, even after all these years.

It was a simple procedure: answer some questions, get a shot, wait for an hour, and leave. They drew blood at the beginning of each session, and again at the end. The shots had made him lightheaded, caused his fingers to tingle, but that was all. But halfway through the eighth week of treatment they began a series of follow-up exercises that seemed to contraindicate the experiment's stated purpose. In these, he was asked to stand in a room and let his mind go blank. He felt the tingle in his fingers then, the tightness in his head. He stood in the room and thought of nothing, tried to put everything out of his head. He felt as if he was hovering, and a white noise seemed to have started up somewhere, a low static sound vibrating in his head. His foot lurched forward, first the right and then the left. He jumped, tried to back up, but he was moving forward, straight toward the wall.

He should have known enough to stop it then, leave and never come back. The next time, he was led into a different wing of the facility, past armed guards and locked doors. He should have run. He still wasn't sure how much of the doctor's influence led him into the that room, into the cage, had forced him to watch while the hypodermic plunged into his arm and the tingling started up, and then the pain settled down like rain.

He had the same feeling now, but amplified. For the first time in decades, he wondered what they had put into him. He knew that whatever it was, it was still there.

Chapter 42

July 9, 1995. Chicago, IL. Soldier Field

Jenkins watched the kid vibrate with the same intensity he'd seen before. "I think I could have stopped him," he had said. It was too late for Crabtree, but maybe not too late to shut this whole thing down. Whatever the kid had in him, it was their best chance.

This is what it's come to, he thought.

Portis was standing twenty feet to their left, the steady stream of Deadheads moving past him like water over river rocks. He held something in his hand, but Jenkins couldn't tell what it was. It didn't seem like a weapon—too small, and he was holding it all wrong if he expected to attack anybody with it.

From the other direction, moving along with the crowd, he saw Tibor approaching. He was walking fast, as always, but too fast, bumping into people, knocking them out of the way, leaving a trail of confused hippies in his wake. This was not the careful old man Jenkins knew. And his face: it was mask-like, something about it...not his. The eyes were dead and staring past Jenkins, over his shoulder, right at Portis.

Chapter 43

July 9, 1995. Chicago, IL. Soldier Field

Pete felt another presence now, something coming from a different direction. Without looking he knew it was Tibor. And he also knew the old vampire cop was in trouble.

In the back of his mind, he picked up a frequency, faint but getting stronger, like snowmelt moving down a mountain, a trickle that would become a gulley and then a stream. There were no words, but something was compelling the old cop forward, an energy, a will that was coming from the professor. This is what he had felt before, he knew, when the vampire had attacked Crabtree. It was why Pete knew it was not the vampire's fault, that there was something else compelling it forward, pulling the strings.

He concentrated, but the old vampire still came closer. He was twenty feet away. Then ten. Pete visualized his own energy interfering with the professor's, pushing the vampire back. Tibor got closer and paused. His eyes flickered with pain and regret and something Pete couldn't place but he knew there were years in it, decades.

The energy was moving the old man further, pushing him toward Jenkins. Pete focused all of his being into breaking the trance. He stepped in front of the old man.

"I'm sorry," Tibor said. He pushed Pete to the side and lunged at Jenkins, stumbled, turned and grabbed the closest person, a teenage girl in a tie-dye with flowers woven into her hair. The old man's teeth sunk into her neck and there were those ripping sounds again, the terrible suction sound of the body torn open and still needing air.

Chapter 44

July 9, 1995. Chicago, IL. Soldier Field.

Jenkins had pulled the stake out of his shorts when the old man paused in front of the kid. Something about the look in his eyes. Jenkins had known him for twenty years, had done more than a hundred cases with him, and never had he seen this look in Tibor's face. He realized the look was fear.

Jenkins felt the wood in his hand. So strange, that this could actually work. In some things, apparently, the folklore was right. Tibor was tearing the girl's throat. All around them, people screamed and ran. Jenkins paused for only a second. He knew what Tibor would want him to do: he took a step forward and brought the stake down in his old partner's back.

Chapter 45

"So where did he go?" Cain said.

"More experiments," the girl said. "Always for him. A way of life, really, if you can believe that."

She was working on a computer, moving numbers around on a spreadsheet. Computers were one thing Cain did not understand. He'd seen the news stories, watched them creep into his radio and television and even seen a few in person as he wandered the late-night streets of Philadelphia or San Francisco or Chicago. It wasn't unusual, of course, that some new thing would suddenly appear in the world. He had been through the sixties. But still, computers were the first thing he just did not understand, where he could feel the limitations of his understanding as certainly as walls on every side—these little boxes that looked like a television and a typewriter at once. What did one do on them? What could the girl be doing right now with her numbers? He didn't know her well, but he thought he knew enough to understand that she would never tell him.

"Are you working on an experiment?" he asked.

"Kind of," she said, her voice indicating she was clearly not paying attention to anything other than what was right in front of her in the screen. "Kind of not."

"What does that mean?" he said.

She made a neutral noise. People could be so irritating. He had removed himself so completely from the normal interactions that he'd forgotten how annoying they could be. People vacillated, lied, made "eh" sounds when you asked them a direct question. He could be behind the wheel right now, driving the van out on some open highway, listening to "Cassidy" or "Sugaree" and watching the little stores and churches and barns roll by. Minding his own damn business.

"If I walked out right now…" he said.

The girl looked up. "Oh, you're free to go," she said.

"Really?" Cain said. He took a tentative step.

"Sure," the girl said.

Cain took another step.

"As long as you're cool staying how you are. With it still in you, I mean."

He stopped. He hadn't really thought about it much, had obsessed over that one moment of weakness, but as for what exactly was making him do this, what had changed, it seemed like no more use worrying that over than the biology of the original change.

"What is in me?"

She closed the lid on her computer and turned to face him. She was really quite pretty, he thought. In another time, another life…But he wasn't that person anymore. He was, well, that was the question.

"How to explain this to a layperson?" she said, leaning back and stretching. "You know that it was the dose. What was in there was…well, it was a combination of things. Really fucking clever, actually, chemically…" she smiled briefly and shook her head. Her tone had changed and she sounded like a teacher explaining something to a room full of graduate students.

"And?" he asked.

"Right," she said, sitting up and moving forward, suddenly animated. "So long story short, two major effects: a kind of tracking component, a *connection* between the two of you. Between anybody, really, whose body contains certain variations, one in particular, of the ergoline family."

"Ergoline?"

"Like, LSD is part of the ergoline family. Where this all started. So everybody reacts to that, right? Or, that's what we've seen. We don't want to say everyone, but it's been twenty years he's been working on this to one degree or another. They've been working on it."

"They?" Cain had no idea what she was talking about.

"Government," she said. "This shit goes back decades."

"What does it have to do with…people like me, though?"

"Vampires," she said. "Right. The other thing is, well, this is the thing we don't understand much about. But it seems that these same synthetic ergoline compounds interact with certain chemicals that only you—or, those like you. Vampires. Certain chemicals that only you have."

"It…what?"

"Well, it's, as I said, really quite clever. With the connection, the mind part, he can stimulate the other part, the part that needs blood, that wants to revert back to what we have been calling 'the natural state.'"

Cain sat down. If he could have cried, he would have. He hadn't reverted back to who he used to be, or worse, to some animal. It had been something else all along. And he had known that, had relaxed and let the current of it carry him along until the bloodlust was sated. But he knew now that he was not that. "Animal," he said. "That's what it felt like. Like a heavy weight was lifted and I was…how did you describe it, again?"

"In the natural state?"

"Natural state," he said.

He let the phrase sit between them. The girl looked out the window. The crowd was thinning, those who wanted to go had gone into the show by now.

"So why are you telling me all this?" he asked.

"Finally he asks the million dollar question."

"Well?"

"I'm not really happy with the evil scientist path we're headed down right now, she said. "I helped you for a reason."

"Did he know that?" Cain said. "That you were helping me?"

She sat back and opened the computer again. "He did and he didn't, if you know what I mean."

"I don't," Cain said. Now he was remembering all of it, how frustrating people could be, why he'd chosen to go off on his own in the first place.

"Well," the girl said. "It's going to have to be enough."

"So what we do now?" Cain asked.

She closed the computer again and checked her watch. She opened the cigarette pack and examined its contents. "Head into the show?" she asked.

Chapter 46

July 9, 1995. Chicago, IL. Soldier Field

Jenkins sat under a tree and watched the uniforms doing their jobs. There were at least twenty of them, another handful of guys in bad ties and cheap khakis. Murder police. Collecting their own data, trying to make sense of what had just happened in their own limited way. He could imagine the gossip. Vampires. Federal agencies. Double murder. They didn't know the half of it.

The kid sat a few feet away. He could have been anybody, some Deadhead wandered into the wrong place at the wrong time, like that poor girl. She was maybe a few years older than David. That sound, skin ripping.

He was two partners down and no closer to getting at the one who had done all the killing, the one who was sick. He knew now, though, that Portis was really who he was looking for, the person pulling the strings. The one who was sick, the one who had killed Crabtree and the others, the biker, was probably just as scared as Tibor had been in those final moments. He wondered what it must feel like, being controlled by something else, someone else, all this time. All that killing. Jesus, he thought, it must be terrible.

So Portis was the one controlling the situation. But why?

"He was coming for me, wasn't he?" Jenkins said.

The kid just stared.

"You hear me?" Jenkins asked.

"Yeah," the kid said. "He was coming for you."

"You diverted him? To the girl?"

The kid turned to look at him. He really was a kid. He should have been going out to bars and chasing girls, applying for shitty jobs or whatever you did with a master's in religious studies. "It's hard to describe," he said. "I tried to block it, kind of. Get in between them. There's a kind of…energy? From one, the little guy who looks kind of like a scientist or whatever, to the other. I could feel it when your friend…you know. This time I could put my own, like, energy into it. I tried to shield him, to stop it, even, but I couldn't…"

"He did it on purpose. The girl. He knew we were armed, knew what I would do."

The kid nodded. He played with his bracelet. "I know," he said.

"Can you feel anything now?" Jenkins asked. In the background, he heard drums and guitars, the old Buddy Holly song "Not Fade Away."

"A little," the kid said. "Almost like a vibration. An aftershock."

"If you got closer to him, it would get stronger?"

"Maybe?"

"And the biker. The other…vampire, the one who killed Crabtree. Can you feel him, too?"

The kid paused. "I think so," he said. "A little. I don't know. I feel something, but I don't know if I should even, you know, with how bad this went, if I should…"

Another siren getting closer. Jesus, did they have to use it? They were going to scare them all away, scatter Portis and the biker and the whole goddamn parking lot to the winds again. An undercover car pulled up and an older man got out. He wasn't wearing a uniform but he didn't need one. He was straight federal, even the Deadheads could probably see that. Jenkins wondered if it was the same suit, or if the man had a closet full of black suits and black ties.

"Nutter," the man said, shaking Jenkins' hand. He nodded to the boy. "Let's talk," he said. "Few things I think you should know."

Chapter 47

Pete picked at his cuticles and stared at the floor mats.

"You're doing a good job here," Nutter said. "We're following. We know what you're up against, or part of it, at least. We're putting some pieces together."

Pete shook his head. "I don't know it's true I'm doing a very good job. People are dead." He thought about the first time he'd seen Nutter, that profile on Glatfelter Hall. He remembered the tingling in his fingers, a feeling like he wanted to go see the man on the steps. Was Nutter doing it, too?

He should have run. It all sounded so crazy, but he'd allowed his ego to be stroked, to believe that he was special, that there was some destiny waiting for him. What would I be doing now, he thought, if I had just said no? Watching television? Doing laundry? Maybe applying to doctoral programs, working through the paperwork in some library. Now people were dead. He had some kind of…connection…to a mad professor and a killer biker vampire. The whole thing would be ludicrous if he hadn't just seen another person's throat ripped out, an old police officer literally shrink up into a pile of ashes when Jenkins staked him.

"Your parents," Nutter said, and Pete jolted. His parents? "You've been told they died in a car accident. That's not exactly the truth." His voice had softened, the first time Pete had heard that tone. It made him nervous. He looked back at the floor.

"One car accident on the Schuykill Expressway. April 21, 1972," he said, the words familiar, like a psalm or a prayer might be, he thought, for normal people.

"What you've been told is not exactly the truth," Nutter said. "They were participating in an experiment. Government experiment. They were agents. Federal. Like you."

"Like me?" Pete said. His mind was reeling and he felt light. The tingle had started up again in his fingertips and he could feel something like static hissing inside his head.

"There was an accident. Controls that should have been in place were ignored. It was a long time ago. This is germane in that it is believed—well, it had been believed and now I feel confident saying that we know."

"Believed what?"

"Your mother may have…your mother did, I believe, pass on some of the biology of the experiment onto you."

"Pass some of…" Pete pulled at the hair on his arms. This was not a dream. He heard the hiss of the nitrous dealers nearby, the jangle of music playing out of cars and boom boxes. He wondered if he could fill himself with enough nitrous to float away, out past the parking lot and the stadium and everything that had happened so far. He wondered what Sunny was doing right now.

"Peter," Nutter said. "You okay?"

He looked at his own dirty feet, pulled at the hair on his arms again. This was happening. He nodded.

"Your parents were involved in an experiment. They were being injected with a protocol, a drug that altered their body chemistry. Your body, your blood, it has some of those same elements. Ergomine derivatives, to be specific. Not that it makes a difference. They're in your, in your chemistry. That's why you can…what would you call it? Sense when these people are near. That's why you are connected to Dr. Portis and the vampire, the one who is sick, the one causing all this trouble."

"He's not really the one causing the trouble, though," Pete said. "You know that."

Nutter nodded. Something in his face changed and Pete wasn't sure if it was the man controlling his mind, putting ideas in it, or if he really felt sorry for Nutter in this moment. "We do," he said.

There was a knock on the window. Jenkins. Pete could tell he didn't like Nutter, something he guessed had to do with different branches of the government, the secrecy of the Invasive Species Division.

"If you two are finished with your big important talk," he said, the sarcasm plain in his voice. "I'm two partners down right now and I'd like to catch some bad guys."

The static in Pete's head had increased, the tingle moving from his fingertips up his arms. His hands were fluttering and he didn't try to conceal them.

"It's happening right now, isn't it?" Nutter said.

Pete nodded. "How does it work?" he said.

"To be honest," Nutter said, "right now, you know more about this than almost anybody on Earth, except maybe Dr. Portis. Or your friend Padma, of course."

Chapter 48

July 9, 1995. Chicago, IL. Soldier Field

"Do you feel anything?" Padma asked. They were standing just outside the stadium, having passed through security but not yet entered through the massive doorways that led into the show. She really wasn't sure what she was doing right now. She had played the two sides against one another for so long that she was maybe coming out on a third side, maybe on the side of this biker vampire who had killed nearly twenty people by her count. Of course, she had set him up with eight, maybe ten. The notes were in the computer.

The biker shook out his arms, wiggled his fingers. She knew he wanted to relax but he actually looked like he was trying to make a bowel movement, something she knew they stopped doing after the change. "Feel anything?" she asked again.

He closed his eyes and concentrated and she knew it wouldn't work. She had read enough test results, seen enough grainy video to know that the ones who have to push would never experience the tertiary effects, would only be able to connect when called, and then only when somebody with experience and power was doing the calling. Unless Peter turned out to be more than what she thought was likely, Dr. Portis was the only person in the world capable of calling the biker.

The band was wrapping up a song she didn't recognize and the crowd roared. They segued into something familiar that she couldn't quite place and the crowd noise doubled. She was always amazed at the crowds, the show inside the stadiums and out, every single night. It had been eight weeks now that she'd been following the Grateful Dead around the country, eight weeks of sleeping in the RV and late-night, real-subject experiments. It had been a month of tracking the biker after his dose, helping him feed, keeping notes in the computer, running what data they could run. In all that time, she was still amazed at these people, these old hippies and young kids and everything in between, coming out night after night expecting a miracle to happen in the form of five aging men with electronic instruments. She had come here an outsider, an agent or a scientist, maybe a little of both, and would be leaving an outsider.

But what kind of agent facilitates murder? What kind of scientist tracks data and simultaneously reports back to a secret government agency on the nature and whereabouts of her subjects? What kind of person takes a subject into a Grateful Dead show in an attempt to track down her supervisor and end the research forever?

She watched the biker struggling. He was no genius, that was for sure, but genius could be tricky. She knew that now.

"You can stop," she said. "You most likely have a limited capacity right now." He looked crestfallen. "And that's fine. That doesn't mean anything, really. It's more about dosage and time than anything else."

The biker relaxed, looked toward the entrance. "So now…" he said.

She wanted to tell him everything would be okay. He had made it, in a way, made it through the change and everything that came next, the doubts and the questions, the answers that led many to suicide or what they had termed "rejection of the self," an embrace of the situation so total that the subject was literally another person after they came to grips with the change. He made it through all of that, in his own weird way, and now he had been brought to a crossroads through no fault of his own.

"I don't know," she said. His face tightened. Maybe he was smarter than she thought. He had made it this far. Why they tended to branch out on their own, to hide, tunnel down into a way of life the way this one had done, she had no idea. A kind of shame, maybe. She looked around at the people coming and going, the constant thrum of the music and the fans and the low hum of the stadium itself, all of it melding together like a single organism, a machine with many gears spinning in different places.

What kind of scientist abandons a project because she feels sorry for the subject?

What kind of agent cuts off communication right when things are getting dangerous?

There were sides on all sides. The biker was waiting for her to say something, to take some kind of lead.

"Let's go finish this," she said.

Chapter 49

Cain followed the girl into the show. He wasn't sure if it was the dose or that term—"natural state." When she said it, he had a flash of recognition, the quick image of the hotel clerk's face—scared and fascinated and something else. Resigned. For just an instant, he could smell the blood, feel the taste of it in his mouth, hot and sticky. He didn't want to admit that it felt good. The girl thought it was shyness, embarrassment, but it was something much worse.

Now he just tried to focus on the girl, focus on the mole on the right side of her neck, watch as it bounced along with her footsteps. The usual din was muted, a dim roar with tinkling in the background that he recognized only as a Weir song from one of the old solo albums. The girl, Padma was her name, he remembered, moved expertly through the crowd, slipping and sliding and winnowing through clumps of people.

He paused and watched the white of her shirt retreat between two groups that he couldn't quite make out, everything blurry and faraway except Padma and that white shirt and that mole steadily retreating. He took stock, held his arms out like a man slowly steadying himself. No vibration. He wiggled his fingers. Nothing. He tapped his feet, examined his arms. He turned his head thirty degrees and tried to focus on the blur of the crowd, honing in on a fleshy shape topped with something red some twenty yards away. Focus, focus, and then it was coming into shape, the rough edges sharpening into a fat biker, shirtless, in a red bandana. There was a blue glow coming off the man. An aura?

He had heard of people who could see these on others but never really believed. The sixties had been enough to turn him cynical about all kinds of things, and the change was enough to cement it in him for good. He turned his focus to the person directly in front of him, a young kid of maybe twenty in cutoff jeans and shaggy hair. He was barefoot but had tan lines on his arms and was still wearing a watch, and a sickly, blood red glow hung off him. Cain didn't know what it meant but he knew it wasn't good.

He scanned the crowd slowly, a kaleidoscope of red blue orange green yellow purple. It was amazing, beautiful, the first time he'd felt truly out of his head since he had made the change. He wondered if it was the dose—of course it was the dose, there was nothing else to account for it. He remembered the dose in his pocket and before he could even think about it he was putting it in his mouth. It felt like something was ending, something was beginning, and he was ready for whatever came along first.

Purple yellow green orange blue red purple yellow green orange blue red. Before the change, he had taken plenty of drugs, more than his share, even, for the Sixties, and he had been plenty wasted but had never had this kind of experience, as if a layer only he could see had been added on to reality. The word came into his head, one he'd only used ironically or spat like a curse: it was psychedelic.

"Yeah, I was wondering what was going to happen if you took that." Cain jumped. He turned slowly, looked down toward that familiar voice, and Padma came into view. She was smiling but shaking her head, too, as if she'd caught a puppy tipping over its water bowl. A blue green purple swirl came off her and he recognized what he was seeing for the first time as pure energy. Good energy.

Cain struggled to speak. "Wha..." he started, surprised by the croak in his voice, the feeling of vertigo from looking down at the diminutive girl. Woman. Scientist, he corrected himself. What the hell was she, anyway?

She smiled. "Jesus," she said. "You should see the look on your face."

Cain smiled and scanned the crowd. The band was playing one of the newer Hunter/Garcia songs, Garcia singing in his sweet, creaky tenor about roads, his guitar lightly noodling flourishes between the choruses.

"Like you're twenty-five again or something," Padma said. "Or, what would that really be? Back to, what, '65?"

Cain looked over the crowd. Everybody was dancing as Garcia shifted the song toward its ending, and the crowd moved like a thousand pistons firing all at once, up and down and side to side and kinking off at crazy angles and all of it moving in perfect synchronicity with the music that poured down from the stage like a rising flood, enveloping them in its warm embrace. Cain was vaguely aware of the girl to his left, of the band on the stage, the rainbow-auraed dancers that jittered and cheered and lay on the infield grass.

Something was pulling at his arm. He felt it lightly and then hard, more urgent, and his brain processed the feeling—*something is pulling at my arm*—before he thought to turn and find out what was happening. It was the girl, of course, Padma, yanking him toward the back of the infield, away from the stage. The drums started in with a New Orleans beat and Cain stopped. "I know you're tripping right now, at least a little bit," Padma said. "And I'm sorry to pull you away from the infield, but we really need to get outside and see what's happening. We really need to find Portis and make this right."

"But I'm…" Cain said, fumbling for the right words.

"You're tripping," the girl said. "Well, that and certain chemicals in your body are reacting to an agent in the drug, kind of opening up, 'becoming actively receptive' is how Portis phrased it."

"Receptive to what?" he asked.

"It's complicated," she said. "For now, the only thing that really matters is you're receptive to Portis, and he is receptive to you."

Chapter 50

July 9, 1995. Chicago, IL. Soldier Field

Jenkins leaned against a tree and watched the kid talking to the federal. Things were starting to make sense, the data he didn't even know he'd been assembling was forming the outline of a crude story. He had been the one to call for an inside man, and he'd gotten it. They just hadn't told him about it, and the man they sent was more of a boy. Fucking government. Still, the kid had been there, on the inside, and he had something, could tap into the same wavelength Portis was using to control the biker. The kid he could work with. The federal was another matter altogether. The guy just reeked of authority, of paperwork and we'll-take-it-from-here. Jurisdiction. Jenkins was used to being the one delivering that particular speech.

He watched the uniforms processing the scene—slow and steady, just like they were trained. Even with the lights going, officers milling around and others asking questions, these kids still streamed through, wasted and oblivious. They'd had to station men at either side of the scene, directing traffic around it like a fender bender. God, he was ready to move on from this case, catch a normal serial killer or a sex offender or something from good old organized crime. The sounds and the smells and the mystery federal agencies, these kids wandering around in a druggy haze, it was all getting old.

He closed his eyes and leaned back, then opened them and prepared to get up, when something registered as familiar in his brain. That sound. A laugh. He stood and looked behind the tree, where a steady stream of people wandered to and from the stadium. David?

The boy was weaving slightly. Drunk or high. He was laughing at something, leaning on the shoulder of a young girl with long blonde hair and a hippie dress. There was something off with the scene, something more than seeing his son in this altered state. Jenkins clung to the tree, kept himself hidden from view as much as possible, and watched the group, two boys he'd never seen before, three girls in shorts and tie-dyes.

They looked so young. Like children dressed up for Halloween. He flashed on images of David: walking into kindergarten for the first time, bounce-houses and birthday parties and travel team soccer. And the boy had inherited so much of Jenkins' own baggage—the too-thick hair and the barrel chest, the habit of walking a few steps behind the rest of the group, even the way he leaned over to whisper to the blonde girl, smiling and shy but more careful than afraid. It was like watching surveillance tape of himself, like hearing his own voice on a tape recorder for the first time.

But it was more than that, too. What was it? What was off with the situation?

It hit him all of a sudden, like a billy club in the gut. He couldn't believe it. Jenkins leaned his back against the tree and listened to the sounds of the group passing close by. He settled slowly, letting the bark scrape against his back, the smile spreading across his face despite everything that had happened on this day. He almost couldn't form the words in his brain, but every piece of the data, every aspect of the situation pieced together to form one conclusion and he knew in his gut that it was true: David was happy.

Chapter 51

Nutter pretended to be talking into the radio, watching the local police go about their business, orderly and fairly calm for the situation. Still, he saw them bunching in groups and knew that if he could somehow make himself invisible and drift into their huddles, he would hear the word whispered like a curse, passed from man to man like an airborne virus: "vampire."

He felt ridiculous, mouthing a report into his car phone, his meaningless words sinking into the government-issue upholstery like smoke, but he needed time. He needed to think. If what the kid was telling him was true, if the pieces really did fit together this way, then the worst-case scenario had come true and the project had changed, or not so much changed as expanded. Now he needed to find the sick vampire and save his own ass, all without actually telling anybody exactly what he knew, what his own role had been in Ultra and Portis and the death of the poor kid's parents, all those years ago.

Jesus, nothing was ever over. He was two years away from a pension and still here he was, sitting ten feet from a murder scene, watching cops joke and sip coffee and whisper rumors about fangs and stakes and silver.

The kid was wandering around, smoking a cigarette and drinking a beer, and Nutter wasn't sure if he was still on the job or checked out and then realized that in either case, his instincts had been right. The kid was perfect for this particular job, and he'd proven his worth more than once already. The fact that nobody could tell that he'd just walked out of an official briefing was pretty much the point.

Jenkins was another matter. He had almost recruited Jenkins and remembered being impressed with the man's file. He'd been a top performer on the partner experiment and if Havranek hadn't gone out the way he did, Jenkins would have been one of the first selected for the project, could have had a real role on this one. But he had done well without the project, had closed his fair share of cases, moved up the ranks on his own, had taken, if Nutter was right, all of the wisdom of the old man and applied it to "straight" cases. Now he was leaning against a tree with a strange smile on his face and Nutter wondered whether he too had gone local, bought a joint or a pill or a bottle and checked out. You couldn't blame him if he had.

But now he was standing up, making his way toward the car. Nutter had forgotten that he was faking a report and realized he'd just been sitting there, holding the car phone up to his ear, staring out at the crowd like a tourist. As Jenkins approached, he put the phone back into the receiver and took out his files. He opened to a page and started writing.

Jenkins got closer and Nutter affected an annoyed air, rolled down the window.

"Is this important?" Jenkins said, indicating the notebook.

Nutter closed the book. The guy was starting to get on his nerves now. He looked awful. Not just the usual grind of the job, but something else, probably the past few days. He had bags under his eyes that were starting to turn black, stubble coming in patchy and gray on his face. The eyes were tired and glassy, an intelligence shining behind them, but through a veil of weariness that worried Nutter. This was their best man on the ground, but was he up for what was going to have to come next?

"What were you smiling about over there?" Nutter said. Sometimes it worked to get somebody off balance, see how they reacted, if their head was still in the game enough to finish.

Jenkins seemed to be considering the question. He put both his hands on the window and Nutter fought the urge to move ever so slightly in his seat to accommodate the altered dimensions between them, but he'd been giving orders for more than three decades and hadn't forgotten everything he learned in his graduate psychology classes. He shifted in his seat, moved a few inches closer to the door, put his own arm on the window as Jenkins retreated.

"Weirdest thing," Jenkins said. "I saw my kid." He smiled again and shook his head. "I should be on the phone with his mother right now. I should be so pissed. I should be…" he stopped talking, held his hands up to indicate that he didn't understand why he wasn't doing any of these things. This was not where Nutter thought the conversation was going to go, but it was useful enough. "But, I don't know," Jenkins said. "He just looked so goddamn happy. Carefree. It was the first time, to be honest, the first time I thought that…" he fell off. "But you don't need to hear all this," he said, his voice moving effortlessly back into the casual disregard of a lifetime policeman. "Sorry about that."

"No," Nutter said. "What were you going to say?" At the very least, he'd have an idea where the guy's head was, if he was likely to cause trouble.

"Ah, nothing, really," Jenkins said.

His guard was back up. Good, Nutter thought. "Okay," he said. "Let's talk about how we end all this tonight."

Chapter 52

July 9, 1995. Chicago, IL. Soldier Field

Pete wandered along Shakedown, stopping every now and then to look at a T-shirt or buy a beer. He smoked a cigarette somebody had handed him, lit, without him ever asking. He hoped it was only a cigarette—Sunny had told him to never accept something if he couldn't tell what it was, especially a cigarette and especially lit, something about doses in the filter or packed into the smoke, but that seemed like a lot of work to dose somebody you didn't even know, and Pete wasn't sure if that would be the worst thing right now anyway.

What could be worse than what he'd seen over the past few days?

What could be worse than hearing that your only real friend was actually a government plant sent to watch over you, to evaluate your potential for a job that only a few people in the world knew existed? He wondered how much of it had been an act and how much had been real. He realized he'd probably never be able to know the answer to that question.

He wondered what else he didn't know, what variation of the truth he'd just been told in Nutter's car. He'd been lied to, one way or another, his entire life, and the only thing he knew for sure was that it would be foolish to take all this information and come to the conclusion that now, this time, finally, he should trust that he was being told the truth. What did Jenkins call it? The data? The data strongly indicated that everything he'd been told was a lie, and everyone he knew had been lying to him about something every day of his life.

He finished a Beck's and put it in a container overflowing with every manner of beer can and bottle. A girl in a flowing blue dress said, "Right on," and handed him a Budweiser. He nodded and continued on. He was starting to feel a little weird and hoped it was just the beer and exhaustion and not a dose. He tried to remember how to get back to the crime scene. Jenkins had told him to stick close.

He wasn't even sure if Jenkins outranked him, who he should be listening to in this situation—surely everybody on the site outranked him in some way, including the twenty or so police who had descended on the scene. He was a rookie and the fact that nobody called him that was just more evidence that he didn't belong—he was a low-level operative for a division that nobody knew about, that had almost no structure, that would send a kid of twenty-four out into an active crime scene with two weeks of training and no way to communicate with his superiors. He had been an idiot to think that this was real, that they had trained him, that he'd been anything other than set up all over again. How did the Dead song go? "Set up, like a bowling pin, knocked down, it gets to wearing thin…"

All along Shakedown, people badgered him to buy one thing or another, beads or shirts or grilled cheese, nitrous and weed and shrooms. He stopped and chugged a beer and then bought another from an old hippie selling them out of a suitcase lined with watery ice.

He was starting to feel the beer, or maybe there was something in that cigarette. All around him the voices were crying out: shrooms doses T-shirts necklaces shrooms doses. His vision was starting to go weird around the edges, as if he was looking through a lens that was cracking along the outside perimeter. He turned his head to the left and the effect moved with him, a brownish yellow tint now smudging his peripheral vision.

In front of him a girl was selling T-shirts imprinted with cartoon characters. Calvin and Hobbes, Winnie the Pooh, Tigger, and Charlie Brown dancing into a setting sun. Most of her shirts were white, but off to the side she had a few tie-dyes, and Pete found himself drawn to a purple and pink one hanging off a wire attached to a branch of the nearby tree. He put his face up to it, smelled it, pulled back, and stared. The purple was so…purple. He'd never seen any purple more purple. It was the baseline, the formulary essence of purple.

"Whoa," he said, and then giggled at the sound coming out of his mouth, scratchy and faraway. "Do you see that?" he said to the girl.

"That one is ten," she said.

He focused in on the purple and then pulled back. Ringing it was a smaller, subordinate circle of pink, its tendrils edging lightly into the purple with a delicacy that seemed hesitant, courtly even. He knew that the purple was female and the pink was male. Interesting, he thought, when you really see it—really see—it's not what they told you it was all along. It's something more, something rooted in the earth and time and history as sure and obvious as a redwood.

This is true, he thought. Finally. Something that nobody can ruin for me. He held the T-shirt in front of him and put it over his head and could feel the purple and the pink falling into him now, like rain, their ancient knowledge seeping into his pores and into his blood, his…what was the system called? Endocrine.

He let the truth of the colors fill him up and he flashed on everything that had happened so far, everything he had learned, and all of a sudden it was so obvious. There was only one person who had been straight with him all along. "If it's meant to be it will happen," she had said, and he knew it was the only really, honestly true thing he had heard in the past month.

From somewhere faraway he heard somebody say, "Ten bucks," and then he felt something poking at his leg and he wondered if the purple and pink were somehow working themselves out through a hole in his leg, but he didn't remember a hole. My ankle, he thought. How could they move through my ankle? What will I do without that truth? He took the shirt off his head and heard the sound again. "Ten bucks, asshole!"

He opened his eyes and noticed the T-shirt girl poking his ankle with a stick. Thank goodness, he thought, it's still in me. He opened his wallet and found a twenty, let it drop on the ground, and wandered back into Shakedown. He kept the T-shirt over his head and allowed the pink and the purple to guide him.

He wandered through the parking lot, noticing the colors. A young guy with dark glasses and a mop of curly hair gave him a high five as he walked past with a group of people heading toward the show. They were laughing and shouting and Pete turned to watch them go. He thought about following them into the show. They were going to have the night of their lives, he thought. It was going to be beautiful.

"Dude. Dude!" Pete noticed that somebody was holding his arm and he wondered how long that had been happening, why he couldn't feel anything along the right side of his body, who this person was who was squeezing his bicep, pulling him back away from the main concourse. He squinted but all he could make out was the hazy figure of a person standing right in front of him, their entire body obscured by what looked like a red cloud. "Pete," the body said. Pete squinted, focused. He could just barely make out a face. It was somebody familiar, somebody he knew. "Oh shit," the voice said. "Now both of you?" He felt hands on his face. "Peter," the voice said. "It's me. Padma."

Chapter 53

July 9, 1995. Chicago, IL. Soldier Field

Jenkins knew there was something the federal wasn't telling him, something missing, a piece of the data that didn't fit with the rest. The guy was nervous. No matter how much he tried to overplay his hand, coming on strong with his, "I don't have time for this," and his devices and official looking reports, the entire time he'd been picking at his cuticles, forming the skin into little balls, rolling them around on his fingertips and then starting again. A tell. A rookie mistake. But Jenkins could tell from the guy's manicure that he hadn't been in the field for some time, that this trip was special for some reason, and it was more than a few dozen dead junkies.

The guy was this close to his pension, Jenkins thought, and still sitting here in a government-issue sedan watching uniforms process a scene. Even if he was here to support the kid, or to pull his element out of the field personally, it still didn't add up. Guys like this send other guys. They don't cancel tee times or dinner reservations to stand around a Deadhead parking lot watching the locals fill out paperwork on the dashboards of their black and whites.

He reviewed what the guy, Nutter, had told him, laid the data out like notecards in his head. There was a federal agency to deal with the vampires. This made sense. If there was an agency to mow their lawns, leave Plasmatrol in coolers on their front porches, measure their body chemistry to make sure they weren't slipping out at night and letting base impulses run wild, then it stood to reason that there was also an agency to clean up when something went wrong. Invasive Species Division. It was cute, he had to admit, to name the division something you could actually put on the front of a building and nobody would bat an eye.

But Nutter was nervous, and he was here, and something about that did not add up. There was something else to it.

Jenkins put the idea away. The picture was forming and this too would reveal itself, he knew, as soon as he was able to assemble the rest of the pieces.

The vampire was sick, or not sick exactly, but being manipulated by Portis. There were three people on the inside, in some way connected to Invasive Species: the greaseball cop, a woman of about thirty, and the Deadhead kid.

The kid was another matter altogether. He had some kind of gift, and Nutter had been vague on the nature of it and the way they'd come to find him. There it was. Why was he being vague about the kid, about whatever his power was? The answer to that question would point toward whatever Nutter was hiding, whatever was actually at the root of all of this, the picture formed out of all the smaller dots.

The ambulance arrived, also blaring the siren despite his specific request that they come in silent. He watched the uniforms finishing up, clumping into groups, no doubt gossiping about what they'd seen. Soon it would be everywhere. Some cop with an axe to grind would call the news, and once it was in one outlet it would be everywhere, and then the vampire and the scientist would scatter to the wind and that would be that.

Jenkins looked around. Nutter was still in his car, talking to somebody on his portable phone, or pretending to. The kid was nowhere to be found. The vampire was obviously gone. The scientist was gone. Tibor was dead. Crabtree had been dead for days.

Jenkins watched the Deadheads meandering back and forth, the ambulance retreating toward the highway. He wondered if David had gone into the show, what he was doing, who those kids were. He had looked so happy. Carefree. It was amazing, really, so amazing he had forgotten to even be angry about it, and he knew that he wasn't going to call David on whatever lie he'd given Kathleen to be here.

David. Jesus, he thought. David was here. Everybody here was in danger. David was in danger.

They were all back to ground, back to whatever had brought them here, wherever they were hiding or waiting or prepping. They needed some way to call them back together, use whatever frequency they were communicating on to get them out in the open.

He knocked on the window of Nutter's government issue. "We need the kid," he said.

Nutter looked nervous. He fumbled with his car phone, put it back in its place. "The kid is gone."

Chapter 54

Padma steered them both to an open space. She really needed to get them back to the truck, back to a safe environment where the biker could be contained and Peter could come down off whatever it was he'd ingested. She tried to make them sit down but both of them were—how would Portis phrase it?—experiencing significant and unpredictable psychedelic effects related to the ingestion of an unknown substance.

The biker had at least tripped before, she guessed, back before he had transitioned. She knew enough about him, or Portis did, to know that he may have even been at the initial acid tests at Kesey's ranch. She thought about that, the biker outlaw passing by the little doctor, then just an assistant professor applying for grants, probably telling himself he was trying to make the world a better place. Maybe the two of them stood side by side while this very same band played in the barn, Cassidy and Mountain Girl and Allen Ginsberg wandering around.

So much history. She would never live through that kind of history, and chasing it with Doctor Portis, with the agency, had been folly. What was happening now, she knew, was the opposite of the Acid Tests, which in a lot of real ways had launched the hippie movement, the Merry Pranksters and acid and the Grateful Dead, the idea that chasing enlightenment in a drug or a bus or books was an option. The Acid Tests were a beginning in a lot of very real ways, but what was happening now, what the Doctor had done with the biker, what Nutter and the Doctor were doing with each other, a decades-long grudge match, it was clear to her now that it was all a waste. It was some kind of ending. Which way it went was still on the table, but she'd seen enough of both sides to know she would side with neither the Doctor nor Nutter. But where did that leave her?

Peter was wandering in small circles. She pulled him close, put her hands on his face gently. "It's me, Peter," she said.

"Padma," he said. "Hey."

"Hey," she said.

"It's all been lies, Padma," he said. "Padma. Pad…ma," he drew the name out slowly, like he was trying out the way it sounded in his mouth.

"I'm going to give you something," she said. "That may or may not have an effect on you, depending on what you've taken."

It was risky, but it was all she could think of. Portis would know the right dosage, what the effects were likely to be. She had paid attention and had enough science of her own to know that this was the best of her limited options.

She held out the dose and he popped it in his mouth immediately. "Oh yeah," he said. "Sure. Suuuure…suuuuuure…suuuuuuuuure."

The biker had calmed down and was laying on his back, looking up at the sky. She sat down next to him and patted the ground for Peter. He sat down and lay back. "Whoa," he said.

The biker sat up. "He's your friend?" he said. She nodded. "And he's not…like me? He's normal?"

"Not really normal," she said. "Special somehow?"

"I could feel him," the biker said. "Before. And now. The same way with the dealer."

"I know," she said. "That's good."

If she could get them back to the truck, she could isolate the biker and get Peter someplace safe. The doctor was not safe, though, and he was probably with the truck.

"Do you remember him?" she said. "The doctor?"

"Remember him? I remember he gave me that dose in Philly." The drug was settling in his nervous system now and the biker was managing it better. "I can't see the auras anymore," he said. "I was hoping that was permanent."

"There are phases," she said. "Kind of almost an overdose, to be honest? The beginning is particularly psychedelic."

"Phases," he said. He lay back down on his back. "Overdose. You have a nice aura," he said. "Yellowy, purple."

She sat up and checked her watch. She hoped Peter would come down soon, too. Her only other option was to find Nutter and the cops and hope they could manage him, but something told her she would be better off on her own. Nutter had his own agenda. Everybody had their own agenda except these two poor

tripping souls who had wandered or been drawn into this situation and still had no
idea what it was even about.

"We'll need everything we have, I think," the biker said.

"What?" she said. "Why?"

"He's coming back."

Chapter 55

July 9, 1995. Chicago, IL. Soldier Field

Eighteen months until the pension. Eighteen goddamn months and then, what? A party, a gold watch, his name on a plaque or not depending on how this last thing went, on how much of the old history got dug up as these latest bodies got put down, processed, and investigated. As somebody started to put together the pieces, the new and the old, until they formed the dotted line that wound over the years between him and Portis. The agency had destroyed most of it in '73, thank goodness, two years before the joint committee hearings.

He needed to get out of this car, do something. Portis knew too much. Way too much. The girl knew too much, too, although he wasn't sure what she would do with her information. Maybe walk away. Maybe threaten a suit. Field operatives were difficult to predict, heady and impulsive. The girl was different, though: smart, thoughtful, reliable. It would be a shame if she had to go away. Putting her with Portis was a risk he thought he had needed to take at the time, but it was another false move, another chain in the trap he'd built for himself.

He got out of the car and motioned for Jenkins. The kid could call Portis. They needed to find the kid. Nutter opened the briefcase and fumbled with the computer. He had no idea if the thing would even work here, in the middle of a parking lot a few miles outside the city. They stood there listening to the low hum of the machine starting up.

"Know how to use that thing?" Jenkins said. Nutter just grunted. He entered his password and waited while a spinning ball danced around his screen. "I been putting in requests for something like that for, shit, two years now," Jenkins said.

Nutter opened the tracking program and watched as the map zeroed in Chicago and then the parking lot. Two dots were blinking: Spot and the kid.

"Holy shit," Jenkins said.

"Tax dollars at work," Nutter said. He looked across the parking lot. "Looks like they're over there," he said. "That direction at least." He started walking and Jenkins followed.

"Isn't there an easier way to do that?" he said, holding up his walkie talkie.

"Chance that Spot quit tonight," Nutter said. "The other undercover. The one who seems, well, like maybe he's gone a little native."

"What do you mean there's a chance?"

"Turned off his walkie. Didn't remove his tracking bracelet, though. Which could mean he's just not thinking or could mean he's tracking the kid, keeping him in sight in case we need him."

"The kid," Jenkins said. "He has, I don't know, some kind of power. Ability?"

"He does," Nutter said.

"How?"

Nutter stopped and regarded Jenkins. The guy was still dressed in his hippie costume, but there was no doubt he knew what he was doing. Jenkins made him nervous. His initial impulse, to keep Jenkins on the case even though he was aware of his history, even though he'd been a part of the goddamn partner program, had been wrong. Keep your enemies close was good advice, maybe, as it concerned politics, but not good police who had the potential to track the money back to the source and see what it was that had really set the entire thing in motion.

Before all of this started up again, he'd imagined the words they would say at his retirement dinner: valor, meritorious, trailblazer, public safety. Now he was one nosy cop or missed opportunity away from the other words overtaking the story of his lifetime of service: mind control, LSD, misappropriated funds, lack of oversight, death, murder, Project MKUltra.

Jenkins ran a hand through his thinning hair. "You know what? Never mind," he said. "Fuck it. I don't need to know and maybe I don't want to. Let's just, I don't know, protect the public safety."

Nutter nodded and continued walking. "Works for me," he said.

"Something tells me you're not going to have the same level of paperwork as me," Jenkins said.

Nutter smiled. "One of the many benefits of not technically existing."

Chapter 56

Pete guessed this is what they called coming down. He felt himself settling down into reality all of a sudden, all the aches and pains and worries draining right back into his veins. His Achilles tendons hurt from all the walking and a blister had started up where his sandal was rubbing against the top of his right foot. He was developing acne on the places below his nose and to the side of his mouth where a thin stubble had been forming for the past week. It was like going from drunk to hungover with no space in between and all he wished for was sleep.

He sat down next to the biker, who nodded and lay back down on his back. Pete realized that he held the vampire no more responsible for what had happened than he would a boulder that had been tipped from its place at the top of a mountain. Was this police work? He had no idea.

"Rest if you can," Padma said.

Padma was a liar. Everybody was a liar. Everything was a lie.

"He's coming back," the biker said.

Pete remembered everything that had just happened to him, in great detail. He wasn't sure if it had been a few minutes or an hour or a day. He wanted to ask what day it was but he didn't want to fully end the spell and it seemed to him that words were the best way to make that happen. It had been real, the entire thing, he knew that as surely as he knew anything. The colors were in him now and they were true.

He wondered if he was really through it. He'd read that you could relapse, that it could alter your brain chemistry. Nutter had assured him that this was just as much folklore as vampires flying, but he also knew now that he couldn't really trust Nutter.

Suddenly he flashed on a vision, a chessboard empty save two pieces in the form of men: Nutter on one side, the professor on the other.

This is what it had always been, all of it, the vampires and the hippies and the experiments, whatever it was that had been left in him by his poor mother, whatever it was that lingered in the hippie and in the old vampire, even the hissing of the nitrous tanks and the sounds from the car speakers—they were scenery in a battlefield, collateral damage in a contest that had been going on for decades.

He lay down and closed his eyes and focused on the color purple, the fact of it, pure and true as the ground under their feet, sure as the moon. He saw his own role, a pawn in the game, another piece moved around, Nutter's agent bearing gifts handed down through biology from murdered mother to unwitting son. Is that who he was? Maybe.

If it's meant to be it will happen.

Pete stood up. He was shaky on his feet. Padma offered an arm and he squatted, waited to regain his balance. It was clear now. So clear. "I'm sorry," he said, looking at Padma while the biker stared. "I have somewhere to be."

Chapter 57

Cain watched the kid walk into the crowd. He was wavering slightly but holding steady. On a mission. He looked at the girl and she was smiling, watching him go. She shook her head and turned to Cain, held her hands up in a helpless gesture. "Huh," she said, but she was still smiling. "I honestly don't..." she said, and then she gave up and just watched him go, the little thatch of brown hair getting smaller in the distance until he blended in with all the other kids walking up and down Shakedown, and then they couldn't see him at all.

Whatever she had given him had lessened the effect of the dose, and as he looked up at her he could still make out a hazy purple aura. He supposed it was healthy, although he didn't have any reason to think so other than the way she smelled—no sign of the rot he could smell on some of the others.

He still wasn't sure exactly what was happening. He would either return to his careful ways, to the person he'd become after the change, or he would end it once and for all and find out if there was anything next. He had never thought so, hadn't even thought about it much at all before the change, but something like the change, like the risks it put him in and the few occasions when the folklore was right, it was enough to make a person think about more than biology. And what he'd done over the past few weeks, what he'd become...he hoped he'd been right all along, that the end was nothing but darkness and sleep.

"It's starting again," he said. The familiar tingle had been buzzing in his fingers for minutes and he realized he was getting used to it, that other than the beacon alert in his head, almost like a magnetic pull, he might not have noticed anything at all.

The girl nodded. She sat down next to him, crossed her legs. "So there are some things you should know," she said. "Especially given that this could be, you know."

"I do," he said. "I mean, I guess I'm ready for a change. You know, ready for this to get better, back to what it used to be…" He flashed on that feeling, standing in the middle of the crowd while the band played "China Cat" or "Women Are Smarter" or "Box of Rain," that feeling of conducting a symphony, of riding an avalanche, in harmony with ten thousand strangers who had nothing but peace and love and joy in their hearts. In the next instant, he remembered that it was gone now, all of it. What was left was like the body of a zombie, lumbering across the country, wasted and mean, gate-crashing and nitrous-sucking and pushing its way to the front of the line. There was a quote he remembered from somewhere: the past is gone, the future is not yet here. All that is left is the present." Something like that.

"If I lose," he said. "And I'm kind of assuming I lose…"

"Wait," the girl said. "there are lots of…

"No, it's okay," he said. "If I lose, will I die? Is this over?"

She sat and thought. He had the impression that she was trying to gauge what answer he was looking for, or at least measuring her response. "It wouldn't be a bad thing," he said, "if that was the case. That's what I'm asking."

She stood up and stretched, looked off in the distance for what he assumed must be the kid. This was not how she expected it to end, he knew. "Getting closer?" she said.

Cain gauged the pull, like an ache in his back. His fingers were buzzing and it had begun to work up to his arms. "I really need to know the answer to that question," he said. His right arm flexed and slowly raised. He tried to fight it but the more he tried to pull it back down, the steadier it moved right up.

"The dose you took," she said. "The extra one. It…well, it would have worked better before Peter left, but—wow, I still can't believe he left." She trailed off, looked in the direction the kid had wandered.

"So this dose then?" Cain said.

"Basically, we just ramped up the amount of receptors in your body and hopefully… Fuck, I mean, I'm not, like, a real scientist." She said the last few words with scare quotes and Cain realized exactly what his chances, what their chances were. Maybe it would be nice to just be over with it, once and for all.

"So that's a yes, then," he said. He tried to speak normally but his breath was labored, it took all he had just to form the words. Pushing them out was like riding a bicycle into a headwind.

"Yeah." She lit a cigarette and watched the Deadheads stream by on either side of them. "That's a definite yes," she said.

Cain felt himself take a step forward, and then another. His arms raised. He tried to speak, to warn her, but he couldn't get the words out. It was like what he remembered of dreams, the bad ones, the loss of control ones he would have whenever he would come down off a bender. The girl exhaled and turned away from him, she took a step and his own steps quickened. She threw out the cigarette and his arms were around her, picking her up, throwing. He watched as she sailed through the air and landed a few feet away, her legs crossed and coming down at a bad angle, a cracking sound, and a scream.

Chapter 58

July 9, 1995. Chicago, IL. Soldier Field

Jenkins let the old federal feel like he was in control, like he was buying everything the guy was telling him, as they moved through the parking lot over to where the man's electronics told them the kid would be. Very little about it added up. If this was a legit operation—two men down, even if one of them was a vampire, even if he was signed out of restriction and hadn't worked for years—the place would still be swarming with CIA. They might call in the National Guard, the way things were going.

But they hadn't. Nutter had shown up, irrespective of the twenty uniforms who were responding to the murder. He had shown up alone and talked to the kid and then sat in his car pretending to file reports and communicate with somebody on his car phone.

Now Nutter was continuing on, filling the air with official-sounding language. He walked slow and pushed confidence out in front of him the way some poker players sat up in their seats when they tried to bluff, literally puffing their chests out.

"Federal jurisdiction is tricky, of course," the guy was saying. "This kind of case. I mean, we've been doing this for years. Decades. I've been on this beat since the late sixties, you want to know the truth. Since this hippie stuff started up in San Fran."

"That long?" Jenkins said. This seemed unlikely.

"There was, what would you call it? Crossover."

Jenkins stopped walking and turned to face Nutter. "Crossover between who? I was in the partner program, remember."

"That time?" Nutter said. "Jesus. Everybody? The hippies and the Hells Angels and fucking rock stars. Heard of the Rolling Stones?" he said. It was a joke but the way he told it just made him sound more out of it. Jenkins had finally found a cop more out of touch than himself. They continued walking. "And the vampires," Nutter said. "They came in from the cold a little bit. The hippies were up for anything—races, creeds, states of being—it was all one big party. But you know that. Everybody knows that."

"Why don't you tell me something everybody doesn't know," Jenkins said. He had a feeling Nutter wanted to talk, to show off, even. You can never have too much data, Tibor had said, and Jenkins had always found it to be true.

Nutter stopped again. He put his hand on Jenkins' arm. "You think you want to know things, but I don't know if you really do," he said.

"I lost two partners this week," Jenkins said. "Try me."

The guy nodded. He adjusted his hat and squared himself as if he was addressing a military squadron. "We started it," he whispered. His voice had changed so much, the surety stripped right out of it, that Jenkins was taken aback.

"Started it?" he said.

Nutter nodded. "Hippies. We started the whole goddamn thing."

"I'm following," Jenkins said.

"You don't understand what I'm saying," Nutter said. "We gave it to them. LSD. We gave it to them. The government. The C-I-fucking-A. We're the ones who started the whole thing. Ken Kesey and Timothy Leary and the Pranksters and the hippies and the Grateful Dead and who knew how fucking long that was going to go on. Who would have guessed we'd be standing here." He waved his hands around at the parking lot and the Deadheads walking, weaving, selling, haggling, dancing and hugging. "Who in their right mind would have guessed we'd be standing here thirty fucking years later?"

"Look," Jenkins said. "I don't know about any of that. All I know is I lost two partners this week. I've seen too many bodies this past month. This thing is sick and it's not getting better."

Nutter shook his head. "So much bigger than that," he said.

Chapter 59

July 9, 1995. Chicago, IL. Soldier Field

Padma stood. Pain shot through her left ankle. She had heard the pop when she landed, even through her scream and the gasps from the kids who were now scurrying around her, retreating to the relative safety of their cars. The biker was pacing, hitting himself in the head with an open fist, muttering something she couldn't hear with the ringing in her head. Every cell in her body wanted to run, to do what Peter had done and be rid of this entire scene once and for all. She was a government employee. What kind of job got you into this situation?

She tested the ankle and pain shot up her leg, all the way to the knee. It was amazing, she thought, how the body worked. Even more amazing was how the mind worked. The biker hadn't wanted to hurt her any more than she wanted to be thrown in the air. Of course, that was what it had been about all along—what Doctor Portis and Nutter had been at the entire time—controlling minds, especially those of the most dangerous. Control a normal person's mind and you could do normal things. Control an extraordinary person's mind and you could do an extraordinary amount of damage.

The biker was coming toward her again, clearly fighting it and not winning. Portis was near. She fumbled in her pockets. If Peter had stayed, she may not have had to do this, but with him gone, with Portis closing in, it was the only choice she had. The biker grabbed her arm and yanked, and then he let go and stumbled away, punching himself in the head again.

She didn't have much time. That was clear. She put the doses on her tongue and sucked.

Chapter 60

Cain concentrated on his arms and legs, on controlling them, fighting the Dealer's attempts to make him harm the girl. She was limping, backpedaling, but not running away. The Dealer was trying to move him closer to the girl. He pushed his feet into the ground and wasn't sure whether he was really seeing his feet move a half inch into the dirt or whether he was still tripping. Maybe this whole thing was just a trip. But he could feel the burn in his legs, every single fiber fighting to stay rooted in the ground, and he knew that it was real.

Letting go would feel so wonderful. He would just relax, let his body do what it wanted to do, let somebody else call the shots, make the decisions for a little while. He would be a vessel, no more and no less. But no, he couldn't think about letting go, couldn't give in to—what was it called?—the natural state. He forced his arms to cross and then held them in front of his chest. He had lifted weights with Angels in Huntington Beach, and the feeling was not unlike a reverse bench press. He had never liked lifting weights.

Portis was getting closer. Soon he would be within view and Cain didn't know whether this would make the man's control over his body and mind more pronounced or less. He felt the pull of his command, heavy like a headache. There was a buzzing in his ears and all he could think about was giving up, that feeling of release, how wonderful it would feel to put down the weight of fighting back, to take that first step, then the second, then sink his teeth into the girl's throat.

He could feel another frequency in the mix—not the kid, not the other vampire, but something else, a weak signal growing slightly stronger, helping him push back, like a small engine at the back of a train. He remembered an old book his mother had read him—could he still picture her face? No. All he remembered was brown hair falling down over her maid's outfit, the way she smelled like cleaning liquid and sweat. It had been a long time since he'd thought of those days.

"Stand down!" Cain opened his eyes slowly, careful to maintain his concentration. If he let it down now, he would be ripping the girl's throat out before he could even register the distance between them. But was that what he wanted, what he should want? The natural state. It sounded like a hippie thing, a goal, the halcyon days of the natural state. Cain had never liked hippies much before the change.

"Stand down!" It was the cop, the plainclothes whose partner he had killed. He wasn't surprised, but when he thought of the partner, he almost lost his concentration and was propelled a few steps toward the girl. The plainclothes was standing between them now, a gun pointed at Cain's temple, a stake tucked into the waistband of his shorts. "There's silver in the gun and the stake I used to kill my partner—the one you didn't kill—and I'm more than happy to use them," he said. "Now just take a few steps back. Now."

Cain forced a step back, then another. He wanted to speak, to explain the entire thing—Portis, the dose, the girl. The girl. She was standing to the side, arms crossed at her chest and eyes shut. She was the other frequency he was feeling, the one that was pushing back, increasing his energy. The older cop in the hat, the one who looked like a federal agent in a movie, was standing near her, shouting a series of orders that she didn't seem to be hearing. He was holding up a folder and gesturing at the parking lot, at Cain, at the plainclothes, as if he was a movie director who was unhappy with how a particular scene was being staged.

Cain felt the girl's frequency increase, layering over his own efforts. In his mind they were merging, gaining power, increasing momentum.

"I will shoot," the plainclothes said. He took a step forward. "I'm going to count to three," he said. "One. Two."

Cain braced for the sound of the gun. That too would be relief.

Chapter 61

July 9, 1995. Chicago, IL. Soldier Field

Jenkins didn't want to shoot anybody. The guy was sick. More than that, even—he was being controlled by forces, Nutter and Portis and this girl who seemed to be on all sides at once. The vampire was responsible for the murders, yes, but in the same way a car is responsible for an accident. Still, he had sworn an oath to protect the public and if that meant putting a silver bullet into this thing and stopping these murders once and for all, or even for the time being, he was ready to do it.

"Sorry," he said under his breath as he squeezed the trigger.

Chapter 62

July 9, 1995. Chicago, IL. Soldier Field

Nutter saw what was happening and did it without even thinking. He wasn't even sure it would work. He focused on the gun, on moving it quickly out of Jenkins' hand, imagined it flipping into the bushes. And then it was happening. The gun flying. Jenkins' hand pulling back as if he was being electrocuted. The gun landing in the very bushes Nutter had been thinking about. He'd done things before, a pen rolling off the table, a spoon bent, a thought put into the kid's head on that first spring night at Chandler University. It had been thirty years studying the art of mind control, five that he'd been actively using the professor's solution without his knowledge. But still, he hadn't been sure it was going to work.

Now, he had saved them a moment, a poor result, but he would have to focus on Portis in order to clean up this mess for the long haul, to get into his pension with a Meritorious Achievement Award and not a congressional investigation. Jenkins was scurrying around in the bushes. The biker was moving toward the girl. Portis walked closer, steadily. He was smiling.

Nutter focused on the biker. He was grimacing, fighting Portis and losing. The girl backed up, one step, then another, slowly and carefully. She maintained eye contact with the biker and Nutter could feel her own wavelength, the curious static that indicated somebody was tied into the energy, that they had the chemicals in their system and the ability to access the connection.

The girl had it up to a point. Her line was weak, fizzling. He guessed that she'd just taken the chemicals. She was smart, but had neither the heft nor the experience to push Portis. She looked back and was making her way slowly toward him. Nutter focused on the biker, on keeping him where he was, moving him back. His progress slowed, but still he advanced, one stagger at a time.

Chapter 63

July 9, 1995. Chicago, IL. Soldier Field

Jenkins fished in the bushes, a mess of beer cans and wrappers and cigarette butts. At any moment, he expected to feel the puncture of sharp teeth in his neck, a bullet in his back. If this is how it ends, he thought, so be it. He flashed on David, that smile. What did they say? Have a good show. He hoped David had a good show, that for once he was able to shrug off the Jenkins family weight—depression, awareness, whatever it was—and just have a good show.

There, nearly covered by a Big Gulp cup, was his service weapon. He picked it up and turned.

The biker was staggering toward the girl, making his way slowly, like a drunk walking into a terrible headwind. The girl was walking back carefully, looping toward where Nutter stood. On a hill, Portis advanced, smiling. Jenkins wasn't sure if he was imagining it or not, but he thought he heard a low electric hum, could almost see the line connecting Nutter to the biker to Portis. The girl was an ancillary item, a spoke that had broken off. She was careful, walking toward Nutter, firming the line between them. She caught his eye and gave him a look, then continued moving the biker closer to the federal.

Chapter 64

July 9, 1995. Chicago, IL. Soldier Field

When Cain had let go, finally, he was surprised to find that he was not moving forward, was not tearing into the girl's throat, but was actually being pushed back from the front with nearly the impact he felt from behind. The result was like stepping through a cloud, a slow lurch forward, two forces conducting themselves through him.

He had tried to make his life on the edge of society, to live among but not with the rest of the world. He had managed for a while, until he made his mistake, and now here he was, no longer in control of anything, reduced to less than the natural state, to some other state where he was nothing more than flotsam blowing through a battlefield, a stake being pushed between two adversaries. He had lived two ways, as a careless man and a more careful vampire. Now he was some third thing without so much as agency.

Chapter 65

July 9, 1995. Chicago, IL. Soldier Field

It was a geography problem, the need to get them arranged in a line. She hoped at first that once they were close, they would conduct through the biker, but that didn't seem to be happening. There was one other way. She caught the cop's eye and nodded. She hoped he would understand.

Chapter 66

July 9, 1995. Chicago, IL. Soldier Field

Jenkins nodded back at the girl. He had an idea of what she was doing, even if he wasn't exactly sure. He hated to do it—the data was unclear, and he had never made this kind of decision without being more than ninety percent sure. There didn't seem to be alternatives. Before Nutter or Portis could push it out of his hand, he raised the gun and fired.

Chapter 67

July 9, 1995. Chicago, IL. Soldier Field

Padma felt the connection wane, a thin pop in the line of what she thought of as static, even though she knew it was something entirely different, something there wasn't a scientific word for yet because the research had been conducted entirely off the books. The biker was down. The folklore wasn't always right, but it was right about silver bullets, and she knew he would not be getting back up.

There was that thin pop, a break in the line, and then what she could only think of as a roar. It happened so fast, the two of them connecting on one another, both of their energy so strong, and then all of a sudden it was gone altogether. She expected an explosion, a massive cleansing fire to be raging through the parking lot, the stadium, the city itself. But all she saw was the two men lying on the ground some thirty yards from one another, each bleeding out of the eyes, ears, and nose.

She saw it all vanish in an instant and knew it had all been folly, the whole thing. It had started as peace, love, and understanding, expanding consciousness, putting the mind past the limits of the body and using science to explore and push through boundaries, and somehow it had all gone terribly wrong, twisted in on itself, morphed, and maybe even evolved into something ugly, petty, and mean-spirited.

She wondered again that Peter had just up and left. It was amazing. She looked at the bodies, the man who had managed to control minds and the one who had carried Project MKUltra off the books and through decades of dark service. And Peter had just walked away.

She thought of Hunter S. Thompson riding his Vincent Black Shadow that night some thirty years ago and feeling like he could see the place where the tide had turned and the sixties had fallen back, like a wave into the ocean. She thought she could see that place now.

EPILOGUE

If I knew the way, I would take you home...
Garcia/Hunter, "Ripple"

August 9, 1995. Ocean City, Maryland.

"Peter!" He could tell from her voice that something was wrong.

He finished drying the plate and put it in on the counter. "Sunny?" She was standing in the doorway, still in her waitress shirt and apron, tears streaming down her face. "He's dead," she said.

Pete flashed on all the people she could have meant: her father, grandfather, either one of her brothers, even their new friends from the restaurant. Somehow he knew it wasn't any of these of these people. "Jerry is dead," he said.

She answered with more sobs, fell into his arms. He held her and cried his own tears, surprised at the emotion welling up and unsure whether it was a real reaction to the news of Jerry's passing, or whether he was responding to her reaction. He loved her. They loved each other, and these sudden bursts of emotion—a sharp pang of love as he watched her brush her hair or talk to her mother on the phone, a deep worry that she was going to wake up and realize how screwed up he was, how much better she could do—still caught him by surprise. He had never really realized how alone he was until he wasn't alone anymore.

"I think we should go to the Reef," she said. He had been looking forward to a quiet night alone, a movie and a bottle of wine and a joint, but he knew also that she would need to be with other people, to feel for maybe the last time that she was a part of the community.

They walked hand-in-hand in silence through the rental properties, and then the convenience stores and beach supply places. Rosko's Reef was a one-story dive bar beneath a dingy realtor's office. "They Love Each Other" was blaring on the stereo and when they entered they saw that Rosko had placed a keg in the middle of the room with a hand tap and a sign that said FREE.

They filled up a few beers and Pete shuffled to the side while Sunny embraced her friend Paige. "He's gone," she said, and they both laughed at the song reference, even as they cried, and then hugged. Pete sipped his beer and stayed to himself and watched Sunny. He was constantly amazed at how deeply she felt things. He wondered if this was how it was for normal people, or if Sunny just felt things a little more deeply. Their friend Stella came into the bar and Sunny embraced her and the two of them cried and wiped tears and then cried again.

"Hey, Pete," Stella said. Pete nodded. "How you holding up, man?"

"He's a rock," Sunny said. "Thank God." She squeezed his arm and kissed him on the cheek.

"I'm okay," Pete said, and he was surprised to find that he meant it. Here, in this beach town dive bar, with people weeping and hugging and quoting lyrics, smoking and drinking and dancing and all of them mourning the loss of a man they had never met, after all that had happened and everything it had revealed, after every step that led him to be in this place at this time with these people, he was finally okay.

The End

Acknowledgments

Thank you, falettinme be mice elf agin...
— Sly Stone

I'm truly lucky to be in a position to give so many well deserved thank-yous!

Thanks to everybody at Pandamoon Publishing for taking on such a very strange project and making it so much better in the process. Thanks especially to Zara Kramer, who opened our first phone conversation by saying "it's such a weird book!" in the most cheerful way possible, and never stopped believing in that weird book, and to Rachel Shoenbauer for such thoughtful and wise editing. Thanks to Laura Ellen Scott for opening the Panda door for me and encouraging me to walk through it.

Thanks to my Barrelhouse family for making such a warm, fun, productive writing community. I love all you good weirdos.

Thanks to Aaron Burch and Alex Higley for reading early, worse versions of this book and providing insight and tough love. Thanks to Sheila Squillante, Becky Barnard, and Matt Perez for all the steady support and laughs that you didn't even know were keeping me going.

Thanks to my parents, Don and Grace Housley, and my sister, Debbie Cooper, for, well, everything.

The only vampire book I've ever read is *The Passage* by Justin Cronin and the character name of Crabtree is a small tip of the hat to that great book.

I would be remiss if I didn't at least say thank you to the Grateful Dead for all the wonderful music and the good times. Thanks to Dave Longaker, Scott Robertson, and Drew Cockley for being my show buddies way back in the day.

Finally, thanks to my wife, Lori Wieder, and my son, Benny Housley. Writing is such a weird, frequently useless, almost always selfish project and I literally could not have written a thing without Lori's love and support and boundless patience. I love you both with all my heart and I'm so lucky we're walking down this road together.

About the Author

Dave Housley is the author of four collections of short fiction, including *Massive Cleansing Fire, If I Knew the Way, I Would Take You Home, Commercial Fiction,* and *Ryan Seacrest is Famous.* He is one of the Founding Editors of Barrelhouse, a literary magazine, small press, and nonprofit literary organization, and is the primary organizer of the Conversations and Connections writer's conference, which is held in DC in the Spring and Pittsburgh in the Fall. He lives in State College, PA with his wife Lori and son Ben. *This Darkness Got to Give* is his first novel.

Thank you for purchasing this copy of *This Darkness Got To Give* by Dave Housley. If you enjoyed this book, please let Dave know by posting a review.

Read More Books from Pandamoon Publishing

Visit www.pandamoonpublishing.com to learn more about other works by our talented authors.

Mystery/Thriller/Suspense

- *A Flash of Red* by Sarah K. Stephens
- *Evening in the Yellow Wood* by Laura Kemp
- *Fate's Past* by Jason Huebinger
- *Graffiti Creek* by Matt Coleman
- *Juggling Kittens* by Matt Coleman
- *Killer Secrets* by Sherrie Orvik
- *Knights of the Shield* by Jeff Messick
- *Kricket* by Penni Jones
- *Looking into the Sun* by Todd Tavolazzi
- *On the Bricks Series Book 1: On the Bricks* by Penni Jones
- *Rogue Saga Series Book 1: Rogue Alliance* by Michelle Bellon
- *Southbound* by Jason Beem
- *The Juliet* by Laura Ellen Scott
- *The Last Detective* by Brian Cohn
- *The Moses Winter Mysteries Book 1: Made Safe* by Francis Sparks
- *The New Royal Mysteries Book 1: The Mean Bone in Her Body* by Laura Ellen Scott
- *The New Royal Mysteries Book 2: Crybaby Lane* by Laura Ellen Scott
- *The Ramadan Drummer* by Randolph Splitter
- *The Teratologist* by Ward Parker
- *The Unraveling of Brendan Meeks* by Brian Cohn
- *The Zeke Adams Series Book 1: Pariah* by Ward Parker
- *This Darkness Got to Give* by Dave Housley

Science Fiction/Fantasy

- *Becoming Thuperman* by Elgon Williams
- *Children of Colondona Book 1: The Wizard's Apprentice* by Alisse Lee Goldenberg
- *Children of Colondona Book 2: The Island of Mystics* by Alisse Lee Goldenberg
- *Chimera Catalyst* by Susan Kuchinskas
- *Dybbuk Scrolls Trilogy Book 1: The Song of Hadariah* by Alisse Lee Goldenberg
- *Dybbuk Scrolls Trilogy Book 2: The Song of Vengeance* by Alisse Lee Goldenberg
- *Dybbuk Scrolls Trilogy Book 3: The Song of War* by Alisse Lee Goldenberg
- *Everly Series Book 1: Everly* by Meg Bonney
- *.EXE Chronicles Book 1: Hello World* by Alexandra Tauber and Tiffany Rose
- *Fried Windows (In a Light White Sauce)* by Elgon Williams
- *Magehunter Saga Book 1: Magehunter* by Jeff Messick
- *Project 137* by Seth Augenstein
- *Revengers Series Book 1: Revengers* by David Valdes Greenwood
- *The Bath Salts Journals: Volume One* by Alisse Lee Goldenberg and An Tran
- *The Crimson Chronicles Book 1: Crimson Forest* by Christine Gabriel
- *The Crimson Chronicles Book 2: Crimson Moon* by Christine Gabriel
- *The Phaethon Series Book 1: Phaethon* by Rachel Sharp
- *The Sitnalta Series Book 1: Sitnalta* by Alisse Lee Goldenberg
- *The Sitnalta Series Book 2: The Kingdom Thief* by Alisse Lee Goldenberg
- *The Sitnalta Series Book 3: The City of Arches* by Alisse Lee Goldenberg
- *The Sitnalta Series Book 4: The Hedgewitch's Charm* by Alisse Lee Goldenberg
- *The Sitnalta Series Book 5: The False Princess* by Alisse Lee Goldenberg
- *The Wolfcat Chronicles Book 1: Wolfcat 1* by Elgon Williams

Women's Fiction

- *Beautiful Secret* by Dana Faletti
- *The Long Way Home* by Regina West
- *The Mason Siblings Series Book 1: Love's Misadventure* by Cheri Champagne
- *The Mason Siblings Series Book 2: The Trouble with Love* by Cheri Champagne
- *The Mason Siblings Series Book 3: Love and Deceit* by Cheri Champagne
- *The Mason Siblings Series Book 4: Final Battle for Love* by Cheri Champagne
- *The Seductive Spies Series Book 1: The Thespian Spy* by Cheri Champagne
- *The Seductive Spy Series Book 2: The Seamstress and the Spy* by Cheri Champagne
- *The Shape of the Atmosphere* by Jessica Dainty
- *The To-Hell-And-Back Club Book 1: The To-Hell-And-Back Club* by Jill Hannah Anderson
- *The To-Hell-And-Back Club Book 2: Crazy Little Town Called Love* by Jill Hannah Anderson

CPSIA information can be obtained
at www.ICGtesting.com
Printed in the USA
BVHW081035010419
544230BV00030B/1849/P